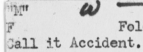

"M"   w ———— 'M.'
F   Foley
Call it Accident.

Call It Accident

A MR. POTTER MYSTERY NOVEL

By Rae Foley

DODD, MEAD & COMPANY

NEW YORK

RED BADGE DETECTIVE

f

Library of Congress Catalog Card Number: 65-21421
Printed in the United States of America
by Vail-Ballou Press, Inc., Binghamton, N. Y.

For George Chapman

The author has never known or known of any real people whose names were those of the characters in this book. The use of real names, if it occurs—and people have been called everything—is sheer coincidence. Nor have any of the incidents occurred outside the lawless realm of the author's imagination.

No personal credit, however, can be taken either for the Grand Canyon or for Las Vegas, although each of them, in its way, seems to exist outside reality.

CALL IT ACCIDENT

1

Mr. POTTER stood looking down at the face of the dead girl. There was almost nothing he could recognize. It was not merely that death had wiped her face clear of expression; the years when her mind had raged and wandered in its special hell of mania had altered everything he could remember of her. There was nothing left, either of horror or of grief; only an awareness, half-ashamed, of the final snapping of the invisible bond between them.

While he stared down at the blank face, the psychiatrist studied him coolly. A slim, blond man in his middle thirties, in fine condition, with smooth and swift coordination. An introvert who had driven himself—or been driven?—into extroversion. No, the doctor decided, Potter was not a man to be driven. The somewhat negative first impression he made was belied by the alert eyes, the firm mouth, the unstressed, unconscious assurance.

Abruptly the doctor nodded to the nurse who pulled a sheet up over the still face. He stood back to let Mr. Potter precede him out of the room. At the end of the sterile white corridor there was a shout, someone banged on a door, and an attendant ran to quiet the disturbed patient. Mr. Potter shivered.

Dr. Holman looked at his watch. "Time for lunch. Join me, won't you? There isn't a decent restaurant within half an hour's drive of here and it's after one." Conscious of the younger man's reluctance, his evident longing to escape, he said, "I'd like very much to have you. Quite selfishly, of course. Now and then it's good to talk to someone as eminently sane as you are."

"Snap judgment?" Mr. Potter asked.

"I'm not infallible, God knows. Sometimes I wonder whether I have learned to look for mental disturbances where they don't exist. But I'm safe in saying you are rather hearteningly well balanced."

In his private suite of rooms on the top floor of the sanitarium, the doctor exchanged his white jacket for a dark one, poured dry sherry for them both, and sank into a deep chair. Mr. Potter prowled around the room, looked at the books that lined one wall, paused before the portrait of a beautiful woman. She should, he thought, have belonged to the nineties, what the Victorians would have called a fine woman—tall, regal, full-bosomed, wearing a dark-red evening dress whose velvet folds had been as meticulously painted as had the diamonds around her neck and in her ears. An anachronism, stately, beautiful, lifeless, "splendidly null."

He came back to take a chair facing his host. On his visits three times a year to the woman who now lay dead in the narrow room downstairs, he had stopped to make the inevitable inquiries, which had grown more perfunctory, more meaningless, as time went on, before bracing himself to pay his half-hour call, always attended by a watchful

2

nurse; to look at the eyes that regarded him without recognition; to leave hurriedly when she became violent.

Up to now he had never really paid any attention to the psychiatrist in charge. He knew that Dr. Felix Holman was highly regarded by his colleagues, that his hospital was exceptionally well run. Beyond considering him to be a cold-blooded fish but efficient, the kind of man who would inevitably have married that pallid figurehead on the wall, Mr. Potter had felt only indifference tinged with the growing distaste and horror that accompanied his visits.

He noticed him clearly for the first time. A tall man of sixty, thin, his dark hair only lightly dusted with gray, glasses that concealed his eyes now that the afternoon sun was reflected on them, full lips that had been disciplined. Too disciplined, perhaps? That might be an occupational hazard.

Holman raised his glass, still looking at Mr. Potter. "To a new life." They sipped sherry in a silence for which the guest was devoutly grateful. He was tired. Well, not tired, exactly. Relieved? No, he rejected that thought with shame. A little lost, perhaps? For eight years he had loved the woman downstairs and now there was nothing left.

The doctor removed his glasses and Mr. Potter saw the weary, thoughtful eyes that scrutinized him steadily and unsmilingly.

"You are cured, you know," Dr. Holman said. "You've been over her for a long time. As you should have been. She murdered how many people—four, wasn't it? Perhaps if we knew more about these things she could have been helped, prevented from violence. Well, we don't know. We keep on locking the stable door. Maybe in time—"

"We'll know enough to see through people as though they were windows? I don't care much for that idea, somehow."

"At least, we might learn to recognize tendencies, to detect weaknesses. But how much do we ever learn?" Holman asked somberly. "Sometimes I envy the young, the half-educated, who are so sure, so dogmatic." Abruptly he shifted the conversation back to the personal. "Yes, you've been cured for a long time. Right now you are just beginning to realize that and you are afraid to know the truth about yourself." He added in the same relaxed manner, "I would say there's not much else that you are afraid of."

"And why should I be afraid?"

"Who knows? Perhaps because nature abhors an emotional vacuum and you don't want to have to fill it up again."

Mr. Potter set down his glass. "Just why are you telling me this, doctor?"

Holman rang a bell and a servant came in to remove the glasses and ashtray. A few moments later he returned with a table set for two. He whipped off silver covers and looked inquiringly at the doctor who said, "We can serve ourselves. I'll ring when I need you."

"It would seem," Mr. Potter commented, an amused gleam in his eyes, "that I was expected."

"After I called you this morning I hoped I'd be able to persuade you to stop for a little chat."

It was a blustering day in late March, the unloveliest of all months in the Northeast, snow piled in dirty heaps between which patches of bare earth were beginning to peer, the branches of trees white and stark against a stormy sky, the wind rising now and then to a high whistle, now and then rattling the windowpanes.

"One thing I'm cured of," Mr. Potter said, "is meddling. Sometimes I wake up in the night thinking of the people

4

I've been responsible, at least in part, for sending to the electric chair, and I get in a cold sweat. No man has a right to play God."

The doctor's spoon halted and then returned to the soup plate with a little click. "I followed the murder case of Eve Grant * in the newspapers recently. Has it occurred to you that Cass and Janet Grant must be rather grateful for your meddling? In fact, I know that they are. One of my nurses, Bertha Christie, used to do a lot of nursing for the Grants and Janet has been kind to her. They lunched together not long ago and Janet told her they owed you a debt that could never be paid. In fact, that's what—" The doctor broke off abruptly.

This time it was Mr. Potter's spoon that was checked, that was replaced. "Suppose you tell me just what it is you want of me."

Holman served lamb, peas, creamed potatoes, passed mint sauce and hot rolls. "Coffee now or later?"

"Now, please. Black." Mr. Potter laughed. "You know we are behaving rather like two strange dogs circling each other." He turned bright-blue eyes on the psychiatrist. "I might point out that I am retiring, as of now, from interfering with people's problems. There is only one thing I want at the moment: to go away, as far away as I can get; to pick up the pieces. When I'm whole again I'll come back and build a new life."

"You're whole now," the doctor said tranquilly. "The pieces have been put together for years. And don't fool yourself, Potter; you'll continue to live the same kind of life. You can't do otherwise without wreaking violence on your own nature."

Mr. Potter was half-annoyed, half-amused. Aware that

* Fatal Lady

Holman expected a protest, he made no comment, placidly eating his lunch. Nevertheless, he realized that what the doctor said was true. He was cured. The woman downstairs had died for him years before and he had not been honest enough to admit it.

When the table had been removed by the unobtrusive servant, Dr. Holman offered cigarettes. "I saw you looking at my wife's portrait."

"She was a Maybrick, wasn't she?"

For a moment the doctor's lean, disciplined face lighted with laughter. "There speaks the old New Yorker. Her mother was indeed a Maybrick but her father was Jake Stendel. Most people would remember that first."

Mr. Potter groped in his memory. "Jake Stendel. Oh, of course; steel."

"Did you ever meet him?"

"I don't think so."

"Then you didn't. My father-in-law was not a man whom you would forget."

"The forceful type, I take it."

"He was the most vital man I ever knew; a short, square fellow who looked like a coal miner, with the impact of a sledgehammer and the manners of a carrion crow. Honest within reason, ruthless beyond belief. He was self-made, aggressive about it, and he wanted five cents' worth for his penny. He married Matthew Maybrick's only daughter because she had what he needed, family and social position."

The doctor pressed out his cigarette. "In a way, I rather liked him. In a way, he rather liked me. Probably because I was one of the only two human beings who didn't want anything from him. We let each other alone, so we managed without too much friction to survive a quarter of a

6

century of being in-laws. Of course, we stayed apart as much as we could. After three days, that endless drive and vitality of his unnerved me. I was wise enough never to test it for a longer period."

Again Mr. Potter looked at the cold, beautiful, empty face in the portrait. Either the painter had been curiously inept or Stendel's daughter had been devoid of vitality.

The doctor followed his eyes. "Jake had two children. Helen, my wife, was the older one; she was all Maybrick. Without the—eccentricities, that is." His tone was carefully colorless.

Maybrick? The name was as old as New York society but Mr. Potter could not—oh, Matthew Maybrick, an old codger, somewhere in his nineties, who spent most of his time at his club where it was rumored that he paid his bills out of his winnings from adroit bridge playing. An eager if tottery diner-out with the few people among his contemporaries who would still bother with him because of his family tradition. There was some other idea conjured up by the Maybrick name but Mr. Potter could not pin it down.

"The younger daughter," the doctor went on evenly, "Winifred, combines the worst qualities of the Maybricks and the Stendels, so far as I can see. Heritage, Potter, is the damnedest thing. The very damnedest thing. A toss-up."

The telephone rang and he broke off to answer it. The impersonal voice in which he spoke made Mr. Potter aware that there had been something more than exasperation in the way in which he had mentioned his sister-in-law. For some reason, he disliked her intensely.

"I am not to be disturbed for the next hour unless there is an emergency." Holman put down the telephone and met Mr. Potter's inquiring eyes.

"I think you had better put your cards on the table."

7

"Yes." Holman sounded tired. "Two months ago, as you probably know, Jake Stendel died in that preposterous house of his on Nob Hill in San Francisco. Heart failure. That's what the death certificate said."

Mr. Potter wanted to get to his feet, to say, "No! I won't be involved again. I'm through with interference; you can't involve me in your problems, in your life." He said nothing at all and, in spite of his inner rebellion, his eyes were bright with curiosity.

"That's what the death certificate said," Holman repeated. "Jake had overexerted for years, but he had the constitution of an ox; I'd have sworn that he would outlast us all. Still—people do go like that." He lighted another cigarette and Mr. Potter observed that there was a tremor in his fingers.

"A week or so later a nurse named Bertha Christie came here asking for a job. We all knew Christie, a hardworking, efficient, unimaginative woman. She's been with the family for years, off and on; always the first one who was sent for when there was an illness or an emergency. Most of the time she was with Winifred who is a hypochondriac, to put it in the most charitable light, especially between marriages, and likes being made a fuss over. Christie is that *rara avis,* a dedicated nurse, and she didn't like wasting her time on Winifred's megrims. I don't think she is really enthusiastic about Winifred, but the whole family has been good to her and she is as loyal as they come.

"Well, Christie had been with my sister-in-law for a couple of weeks—Winifred and her current husband, James Lawrence, lived at Jake Stendel's house—at a time when Jake had an attack of influenza and severe lumbago, so Christie took charge of him. There was a doctor in attendance, of course."

8

Holman pressed out his cigarette impatiently, went to look at the threatening sky, the grimy snow. The prospect did nothing to cheer him.

"After Jake's death, Winifred urged Christie to take a long vacation, a slow freighter somewhere, so she could rest up. She gave her the money for it, though Winifred is not a generous woman, but she knew that Christie is an impassioned sightseer. However, as I said, Christie likes nursing. Instead of going away, she came to me. Of course I took her on. There are never enough nurses."

He came back to his chair, reached for another cigarette, changed his mind and pushed the box away irritably.

"Two weeks ago, Christie asked to speak to me. She said that something had happened and she wondered—so help me God!—if she ought to mention it. She said"—the doctor's voice checked and then went on steadily—"that the morning after Jake's death she had cleared his room. There were indications of vomiting and diarrhea. A glass beside the bed was empty except for a slight sediment in the bottom. That glass had not been there when she left her patient the night before, so it had come from an unknown source.

"Well, Christie knew damned well that something was wrong. She removed the glass and cleaned up the room before the doctor came. He issued the death certificate without hesitation, but he'd been past the age of retirement for some time and Jake had given a lot of money to help him treat some special cases. Christie had been with the family for years and she was truly grateful to them, but she is a nurse first; she thinks like a nurse. She took the glass to a druggist who had the stuff analyzed. White arsenic."

"Were the symptoms you described characteristic?"

"Oh, yes. Well, Christie broke the glass but it has been

increasingly on her mind, driving her crazy, wondering—which one." His voice trailed off for a moment. "So she dropped the package in my lap."

"Was Stendel buried in San Francisco?"

"Cremated, but that was by his own instructions."

"His family was aware of his wishes in the matter?"

"Oh, yes, of course."

"Convenient, wasn't it? So there's no evidence."

"Not a scrap."

"Have you been in touch with Stendel's physician?"

"He was killed in an automobile accident the morning Stendel was found dead. His brakes failed when he was leaving the house, going down Nob Hill. Do you know San Francisco?"

"I do. And those hills!"

"So you can imagine the ghastly mess. He went down, out of control, hit another car, careened into a third; result, three deaths, a couple of children badly hurt, multiple injuries for other passengers."

"His brakes failed." Mr. Potter's voice was quiet.

"That's what the papers said at the time."

"It's quite a story, isn't it?" The question, casual in tone, gave Dr. Holman a feeling very like despair. Then he saw the expression in the eyes that watched him. "Has Miss Christie discussed this with anyone but you?"

The doctor's tension relaxed. He had caught his elusive bird in the net of curiosity. "She says not and that is good enough for anyone who knows Christie."

"But, of course, someone must know that she took the glass away." When there was no response, Mr. Potter asked, "Why did she break down and tell you after so long a time?"

"I don't know. Conscience, probably. Or fear. She has

been part of the family for years. In fact, she has been with Winifred, off and on, during all four marriages. You knew Winifred had been married four times?"

Mr. Potter confessed that he did not follow the society columns with any sustained attention and the doctor laughed without amusement. Winifred was front-page stuff. She had eloped with a Georgian prince when she was seventeen. That one ended in a Reno divorce. He had died since, after several more matrimonial misadventures. Her second husband was Theodore Morris, about whom Holman knew little and cared less. All he was sure of was that the marriage had been of short duration. The third husband was Damon Knox, a movie actor and father of her only child, a son Damon. He'd met the man a few times. One of those repellently handsome men. She had got that divorce in Paris.

Mr. Potter looked up, alerted by something in the doctor's voice. The man was trying to be impartial, detached, but he could not conceal his dislike for the actor.

The fourth husband was James Lawrence, the only one of the lot who was worth powder to blow him up or who had been able to keep Winifred on an even keel.

"What do you want of me, Dr. Holman?"

"Winifred has just learned that Christie didn't take her vacation, that she is working here instead. She called long distance and practically demanded that Christie come back to her. She says she needs her, that her nerves are all shot to pieces."

"Well?"

The doctor made an irresolute gesture. "Christie always responds to a call from the family; I can't prevent her from going. But, my God, man, suppose she unburdens herself to the wrong person?"

"You're telling me, aren't you," Mr. Potter said evenly, "that you believe your sister-in-law murdered her own father."

The blunt words brought the doctor's chin up with a jerk, as though he had not dared as yet to be explicit about his own meaning even to himself.

"One of the family did, Potter. I don't know which one. But I can't go on without knowing the truth."

There was no sound in the room for a long time while Holman studied Mr. Potter's unrevealing face, looking for some indication of what he was thinking.

At last the latter asked, "Who inherited?"

"The estate hasn't been settled yet. Jake had enormous holdings, you know, all over the place, both here and abroad. It may be months before the whole thing is wound up. Helen has been dead for five years, so the residuary estate is divided equally among Winifred and the two grandsons, Winifred's boy and mine and Helen's, though Jake put in a lot of qualifying, not to say threatening, clauses. He was good at that sort of thing."

"Threatening?"

"You know the kind of hold a man like that wants to have on his dependents: 'As long as they bring no dishonor on the name I have established through my own efforts.' One of those watch-your-step-or-else warnings to make them toe the mark."

"Winifred knew about the provisions of the will?"

The doctor gave a bark of laughter. "We all did. He read it aloud to us the day he signed it."

"When was this?"

"Late in the fall some time. November, I think. I was out there for a medical convention. Had to read a paper."

"Go on."

"Well, there's a big enough settlement to keep Christie

in comfort for the rest of her life, if she wants to stop working, which she won't; and smaller sums for secretaries and
servants who have been with him over a period of years. A
lot to charities of various kinds." Holman smiled wryly.
"Nothing for medical research or hospital beds, naturally.
Quite a big slice to old company employees; a block of
stock to some executives of the organization."

"What about the sons-in-law?"

"Oh, we're out of it," Holman said cheerfully. "When
the girls married, Jake made it clear he wasn't supporting
their husbands, then or later. That was fine with me,
which was why Jake and I got along. He couldn't interfere
with me or my profession or my wife." For a moment his
eyes rested on the lovely, empty face on the wall. "It was
all right with Helen, too. She found being a Stendel rather
oppressive and I got on my feet early in my career. She was
a happy woman in a placid sort of way, the way she wanted
it."

"Who has the job of interpreting Stendel's wishes and
determining whether or not his name has been dis-
honored?"

Holman grinned. "Roland Adams, the executor." His
grin broadened. "I told you there were only two people
who didn't want anything from Jake. Adams is the other
one. He had no use for Jake and never concealed it. As a
result, Jake trusted him more than any other person he
ever knew."

"Was he justified?"

The doctor laughed outright. "Adams looks like a combination of a bust of Cicero and a caricature of a thin-
lipped Vermonter. He's incorruptible. He's inhuman. He
holds the scales of justice in his hands but he's not blind-
folded. Not R. A. And those initials are usually inter-
preted as meaning Recording Angel."

"He sounds formidable. Why haven't you taken up this peculiar situation with him?"

"I did. At once."

"And?"

Holman shrugged. "R. A. doesn't give anything away. I simply don't know." His hands closed over the arms of the chair. "Well, Potter?"

"You want me to go to San Francisco, is that it? To keep an eye on Miss Christie?"

"No, the family has been in or near Las Vegas for nearly six weeks. If he had known, Stendel would have raised a howl that could be heard across the continent. Gambling was one of the things he most hated. Winifred said they would drive to Arizona—Flagstaff, I think—and pick up Christie, who could take a plane there from New York. They would show her Grand Canyon. As I told you, Christie loves scenery. That's why it must have been hard for her to turn down that cruise. Her only abiding passions are nursing and photographing scenic spots."

"They? Winifred and her present—fourth—husband? James Lawrence, you said?"

"And Winifred's son, Damon Knox. And," Dr. Holman added, "my son Burgess. To my considerable surprise the cousins have spent a lot of time together lately, though they loathed each other when they were younger; partly, I suppose, because they are so completely unlike. Heredity is full of surprises."

It was the second time Holman had harkened back to the subject of heredity. Mr. Potter was thoughtful. "I— see." After some time he asked, "Was your son Burgess in San Francisco two months ago?"

The doctor nodded. "You understand now why I have to know the truth."

2

JOHN WESTON was tall and thin. Although he was only in his middle thirties his sandy hair was already receding. Through thick-lensed glasses his eyes peered out with an owl-like solemnity; they, together with his conventionally cut but baggy suit, made him look like a college professor. His sardonic expression and general air of being surprised by nothing lent him the appearance of a political reporter. His smooth line of patter made him sound like a television announcer reading a pitch.

Actually he was a lawyer who had begun to make a name for himself as a special investigator for the district attorney's office, had been forced to resign because of a prolonged illness, and was at present, considerably to his own surprise, a private detective. He found the job mildly amusing because he did no more than would provide him with basic support, leaving him free for the pursuit of his interests, which were many, and the fostering of his prejudices, which were acute.

As Mr. Potter opened the door of the Weston office in a high and profoundly uninteresting building at Fifth Avenue and Forty-second Street, the detective spoke without looking up.

"Positively no divorce cases."

Mr. Potter grinned, pulled out a shabby chair beside the desk and sat down. Weston continued to work for a moment, put down the bit of charcoal and looked up.

"That's not bad," Mr. Potter commented, studying the figure of the running man, caught in a few bold strokes.

"It's damned good," the detective retorted. When he leaned back in his chair, legs stretched out, there seemed to be a lot of him, about six feet four and narrow as a knife blade. Behind the thick glasses he blinked myopically at the newcomer. "I've seen your pan before—in the papers." Mr. Potter winced. "You're the guy who finds corpses." Vertical lines deepened in the thin cheeks when Weston smiled. "Well, well, if I'm getting involved with you I can hear opportunity knocking at the door. Go away, opportunity. I'm a lazy man. I don't like work. And if half of what they say about you is true—"

"Never believe more than half you hear," Mr. Potter advised him.

"Brother, I learned that at my mother's breast. Say on, I'm all ears. How did you hear about me?"

"O'Toole. He said you have a certain rudimentary intelligence when you care to use it and you'll take a job if it interests you."

"Go on and interest me. But I warn you that I've paid the rent and there's enough left over to live on for six weeks, so it had better be good."

"The ambitious type," Mr. Potter commented to no one in particular, "straining every nerve to reach the top of the ladder."

"I'm a ball of fire," Weston told him lazily, "but there's no point in being an extremist. I sit here seeing life steadily and seeing it whole. I gather moss. Very underrated product, moss." He pushed aside the sketch, reached for a notebook, unscrewed his pen. "O'Toole being our handsome lieutenant of homicide, I take it that you are mixed up in another murder. Past or future?"

"Both, possibly; possibly neither. Ready?"

"Go ahead."

Mr. Potter went ahead. Weston made comparatively few notes; now and then he peered owlishly through the thick glasses, but for the most part he simply listened. At length he put down his pen and leaned back.

"You do get yourself involved in the damnedest situations. I can see now why O'Toole once said that he never knew whether you just stumbled into things or whether you made them happen." The grin faded while he looked over his notes. "This is a little stinker. Not a scrap of evidence. Nothing but the word of that nurse and a lot of wild conjecture. May be nothing in it at all."

"But we can't take a chance on the nurse," Mr. Potter pointed out. "Damn it, man, she's a sitting duck."

"What do you want me to do—be a bodyguard?"

"No, I think I'll handle that part of it myself."

"How are you going to manage if she's not willing to go along with you on this?"

"I'll play it by ear. Something usually happens," Mr. Potter said vaguely.

"Yeah, that's what O'Toole told me, that you make things happen. A catalyst."

"What I want you to do, Weston, is to dig up background stuff. I want all you can get on Stendel, his organization or network of organizations, and his family: his daughters, his sons-in-law, his grandsons. I don't know what I'm looking for so I can't give you any more specific directions than that."

"There's the will with the implied threat."

"There's that," Mr. Potter agreed.

"And the brakes that failed on the doctor's car."

"Are you interested?"

"I'm interested but I don't know how far I can get with the financial end. I have no good sources with that kind of inside track."

"My banker will do what he can for you, open doors and all that; possibly he can provide a few leads. Oh, there's a chance I can get a line myself on Winifred's third husband, the actor, from Graham Collinge. May I use your phone?"

After a few moments' wait the famous playwright's voice blasted so loudly over the telephone that Mr. Potter held it away from his ear and the detective could overhear every word.

"Hiram? I hoped I'd heard the last of you."

"Now look here—"

"Every time you show up you mean trouble. You're like the shadow of a buzzard hovering over a man dying of thirst in the desert."

"Very moving prose," Mr. Potter congratulated him, "but inaccurate. As I recall, you're the culprit who lured me into the last one."

"God forgive me! All that reconciles me to that business is that you saved Cass Grant from the chair and his sister Janet from being strangled. I finally managed to ply her with liquor last night but all she talked about was you. She asked if I ever saw you and I said not when I could help it." He was half laughing, half serious. "If you've forgotten her phone number—or is there something else on your mind?"

"Something else. Did you ever hear of an actor named Damon Knox?"

"Sure. Movies. He was at his peak about twelve years ago."

"What do you know about him?"

"Not much. He was a handsome devil, which was his downfall; professionally, at least. He could have been one of the really great actors but he got typed in Hollywood as a kind of Cary Grant and he couldn't break away from the debonair-hero roles. And women fell for him. Man, did they! He married one of the Stendel girls—the homely one, too. There was a big breakup and she got a divorce."

"Give, man, give!"

"I don't really know anything else," Collinge said. "Oh, rumors, of course. Always rumors in show business. Story was that she paid him off. Must have been plenty because he stopped acting and disappeared. There was some vague talk about him living abroad somewhere. Probably caught himself another rich woman. Too bad because he could have been an Albert Finney. Really big stuff, I mean."

"What do you know about his wife?"

"New York society is not my beat," Collinge pointed out, "and if the Maybricks weren't old New York society, nobody is. Old Matthew is still around. Eccentric as hell, like the whole family. Fantastic the amount of vitality some of those old birds have. Now and then I run into him. He has already outlived his daughter by nearly a generation. She married Jake Stendel."

"Did you ever know his granddaughters?"

"Slightly. Helen was the beauty. She married Felix Holman, a neurologist or psychoanalyst or some damned thing. Met them a few times. Winifred started her career by marrying a prince. Always marrying some fellow or other. I don't know just when she picked up Damon Knox. Restless girl. Settled down now, I understand. Lawrence, her present husband, seems to have a steadying effect."

"What's he like?"

"Easygoing and no nerves; which is just as well; Winifred has enough for both. Useful word, nerves, isn't it? Covers a multitude of sins. Lawrence is a sound businessman but not a power-seeker like old Stendel. From what I've heard, he's all right.

"You know, Potter, you've got a better source on the family than I have. Both the cousins, Damon Knox and Burgess Holman, used to hang around Janet Grant. Before the trouble, of course. But then most of the available young men did. She could tell you more about them than I can."

While Mr. Potter listened, the detective studied his new client. Potter wasn't the dilettante, the dabbler in crime for sensation's sake, that he had gathered from the press. Far from it. None the less, Weston was aware of a hard core of toughness. Potter hated violence but he could not ignore it; something in him had to fight it.

"Did you get all that?" Mr. Potter asked when he had put down the telephone. "Collinge sounded as though he had just opened the window and bellowed at me. Well, Knox looks like one name we can scratch off the list."

Weston nodded, opened a desk drawer and pulled out a bottle of bourbon and a couple of paper cups. "I don't really like this stuff much but private eyes are always supposed to keep it cached away, and as long as I'm making like one—" He poured drinks and pushed one toward Mr. Potter. Then he reached for a stick of charcoal and did a quick rough sketch of Graham Collinge, mouth wide open, calling from his window.

"This Miss Grant," he said casually, eyes on his drawing, "sounds like a good bet. Might get some leads there."

Mr. Potter drank slowly. There seemed a general conspiracy to make him see Janet Grant again. According to Dr. Holman she knew the nurse, Bertha Christie, and kept in touch with her. Both of Stendel's grandsons had paid attention to her. Considering that she had been regarded as the most beautiful debutante in a generation there was small cause for wonder in that. As their contemporary she would be bound to know far more about them than their elders did.

It was essential to call her, ask what she could tell him. Be better to see her, of course. In an unhurried conversation things came out that one would not think of saying over the telephone. Dinner, perhaps. He was startled to realize how vividly he could remember every detail from the long black eyes under tilted brows to the pale-gold hair that provided such a startling contrast. It was disconcerting to discover how much he wanted to see her again, because he had no intention of doing so. That door was closed.

There had been an unexpected moment when he had lost his head over her, and he had withdrawn in a kind of confused loyalty to the woman who had died in Dr. Holman's sanitarium that morning. Or was Holman right in saying that he was afraid of emotional complications? Confound the man, anyhow!

Janet had responded at the time in a way that had shaken him, but Janet, he reminded himself, had been in a dangerous position and he had been her only support. He did not want her gratitude and there would be no way of making sure that gratitude did not provide the springboard for her feeling for him. Better to stick to his original decision and stay as far away as he could.

When he had left the detective, after making arrangements for expenses and reports, Mr. Potter went to look through a viewer at the public library's old newspapers on microfilm. Jake Stendel's death had warranted headlines but most of the reports were devoted to the steel man's spectacular career, the building of his powerful organization with its many ramifications, and his colorful personality.

The automobile crash in which Stendel's physician and two other people had been killed had rated only a couple of sticks of type. Probably there would be more information in the San Francisco papers. Mr. Potter made a note to query Weston on this, though he was inclined to believe that, in spite of the detective's emphasis on his incurable indolence, he was a self-starter who would require neither guidance nor prodding.

Winifred Stendel had managed to make the front page at frequent intervals. Her elopement at the age of seventeen with a Georgian prince and her flamboyant divorce from him had been played up exuberantly. So had her marriage to Damon Knox, the actor. If the photograph of the latter was reliable, he was an extraordinarily handsome man. Standing beside him, Winifred looked insignificant but inordinately pleased with herself. She had no trace of her older sister's beauty.

Mr. Potter studied the wedding picture for a long time. This was the woman whom Dr. Holman suspected of poisoning her father, this woman or his own son. Mr. Potter had a chilling conviction that if the doctor were to be sure of his son's guilt he would not lift a finger to save him. In his own way, Holman's clinical detachment might be as ruthless as Jake Stendel's drive for power.

After a boring dinner with his banker, to whom he gave veiled instructions without revealing the reason for the information he required, Mr. Potter made a series of telephone calls to find out what, if anything, was known about Matthew Maybrick, Jake Stendel, the latter's daughters, their husbands, their sons. Because of his frequent association with crime he discovered in dismay that even his close friends were evasive and disinclined to commit themselves. They didn't, they explained in various ways, "want to get involved in anything."

By ten o'clock that night he scratched the last name off his list and looked thoughtfully at his meager notes. You couldn't, he decided, fight fate. He must open a door that he had firmly closed. The only source of information left was Janet Grant.

He didn't, after all, find it necessary to make excuses for his long silence, to explain why, after so many months, he was calling her again. There was so much honest gladness in her voice, so undemanding a pleasure in hearing from him that he wondered, in some surprise, just what he had been afraid of.

"Cass wants to know when you are coming to see us," she said after a few moments of idle talk. "Soon, we both hope."

"I wish I could but I'm up to my chin in last-minute details," he told her. "I'm driving west in a couple of days, Grand Canyon and Las Vegas."

"Oh." Her voice was flat. Then, with an effort, it was gay again. "You've got involved in something, haven't you?" She added hastily, "You needn't tell me, of course, except—how we can help."

His question surprised her. No, she couldn't tell him

much about Damon Knox or Burgess Holman. She hadn't seen either of them for four years. She did not ask why he wanted to know about them.

"Well, it was just a chance. I understood you knew them fairly well."

"But it was so long ago, Hiram. They were among the first to drop out when Cass was arrested for murder. I'm sorry I can't help."

It wasn't important, he assured her. No, he had no idea how long he would be away. Yes, twenty-five hundred miles of driving could be tiresome, particularly if these early spring rains were to continue.

"You could do it in a few hours by plane," she pointed out. "By chance I was lunching not long ago with the woman who nursed my father in his last illness and who still does nursing for Damon's mother, Mrs. Lawrence. She's flying out to Grand Canyon in a few days, and scared to death because it is her first flight."

"Oh? That's Miss Christie, isn't it?"

"Yes, and don't try to tell me that she is in any trouble. People like Bertha Christie are born to salvage the ones who get into trouble. I can't imagine anything happening to her."

"I hope," he said, "you are right," and was appalled at his own lack of discretion.

Even then, Janet asked no questions. "Nothing must happen to Christie," she said firmly. "She is one of the world's really good people. You take care of her, Hiram."

3

On the pennsylvania, Ohio, and Indiana turnpikes, Mr. Potter encountered comparatively little traffic except for the huge transcontinental trucks that thundered by, day and night. The roads were icy that unseasonable spring and sleet kept forming on the windshield. When he stopped for food or to refill the gas tank, he wondered bitterly why he had let himself in for this sort of thing. In such weather even animals had sense enough to take cover.

What drove him into these situations? He told himself bitterly that he was a quiet man and all he asked was a quiet life. But the essence of a quiet life was a withdrawal from trouble, and no one with an adult sense of responsibility could keep clear of involvement with, of commitment to, his world. Actually there was no choice.

The first night he found a motel with a bar and a reasonably good restaurant. After refreshing his memory by a look at the map to get the following day's route clear, he checked his mileage. Three hundred and eighty miles.

Certainly not good, but not too bad considering the condition of the roads, the poor visibility, and the long patient intervals when he had crawled behind sanding trucks at ten miles an hour.

Before going to bed he put in a call for John Weston. It was eleven o'clock and he felt a moment's compunction, but the detective sounded alert when he answered and gave his report briskly. He had dug up quite a bit on Jake Stendel.

"But nothing that shouldn't be there. Nothing out of the way at all. He was tough as they come but honest enough. In a legal sense. That is," he elaborated, "if you can afford the right lawyers."

Mr. Potter laughed. "Anything else?"

"What Dr. Holman told you about the will checks with my findings. The bulk of the estate is divided three ways: Winifred Lawrence, her son Damon Knox, and Dr. Holman's son Burgess. Of course, there's nothing to prevent Winifred from turning over what she gets to someone with the right touch of persuasion but—"

"Well?" Mr. Potter prodded.

"If she's the openhanded type, there's not a trace of it. No heavy payments to the guys she divorced, for instance; not the usual pattern of the heiress paying off the fortune hunter. Nothing I've been able to turn up jibes with Collinge's story that she paid off her third husband, Damon Knox. Her motto seems to be, 'Never give a guy an even break.' And there's another thing: that word 'dishonor' in the will was more than a word to the wise; it could be a bombshell if anything crops up before the estate is settled."

"That's interesting. Anything specific?"

"Just casually dropped hints about the Maybricks, a

strain of—well, call it queerness—runs through the family. A bunch of oddballs. Old Matthew had a sister who lived 'retired'—nice Victorian euphemism, isn't it?—and was kept out of circulation. Further back it's hard to get anything you can count on. Families clammed up on that sort of thing."

"Keep digging, will you?"

"Another thing. Winifred's son, Damon Knox—I get a funny smell there."

"What's wrong with him?"

"I can't put my hands on anything tangible. He wants to be an actor like his father and he seems to have the stuff, but when he lands a television job something always comes unstuck. Rumors."

"Mental instability? Unreliability?"

"I can't get anything clear cut," Weston sounded exasperated. "Just raised eyebrows and shrugs." He went on, "The other daughter's husband, Dr. Felix Holman, the one who involved you in this mess, has a solid reputation; brilliant, in fact. People come to him from all over the world. He has a good sanitarium and a big income. Nothing there. His son Burgess is a different kettle of fish."

"What kind of fish?"

"Pickled," the detective said succinctly. "He bends the elbow. He gets tossed out of bars. He gets picked up as drunk and disorderly. He lost his driving license because of a hit-run case when soused. Started early. Kicked out of college for running down a guy who lost an eye as a result of the accident. Quite a lot of feeling about it and his mother spent plenty hushing up the case. They tell me he's one of those thwarted geniuses."

"Genius at what?"

"I wouldn't know," Weston admitted. "Apparently he

thinks he is a composer. The other school of thought, which includes everyone but Burgess, thinks he is not a composer. Some new kind of music, more fury than sound. I get a kind of undertone that indicates the 'dishonor' clause in the will might have been put in for Burgess's benefit. In other words, he may find himself left high and dry. Well, high at any rate."

"Anything else?"

"Hell, man, there's only one of me and a lot of people to check on, most of whom are far, far from Manhattan. Oh, I picked up a bit on Winifred's second husband Morris. Quite a job getting a line on him. The marriage was very hush-hush, probably because the first one had made so much noise. Didn't last more than a couple of years, apparently, and while it did they lived out of the country most of the time. Actually, very few people seem to be aware of that marriage. So far as I can make out, she didn't inform her father."

"He never knew about it?"

"I wouldn't say that." Weston was cautious. "Stendel had ways of knowing what was going on. Not the man to have the wool pulled over his eyes. Certainly not by a screwball like Winifred.

"Well, next thing we know she is back in circulation again. This time she caught herself Damon Knox."

"Nothing else about the second guy, the one she kept under wraps?"

"Well, yes, I discovered he's Teddy Morris, known in certain circles as a professional gambler. Worked the tables from Mexico to Monte Carlo, and from Reno down to Las Vegas. That's where he is now, by the way. He goes where the pickings are good."

"Las Vegas!" Mr. Potter was startled. "How long has he

been there, do you know?"

"I'll try to get it in time for your next call. My impression was that he's a comparatively new arrival on the Strip. Oh, one more thing. The fourth husband, James Lawrence, is a real-estate man in California. Well liked. People speak of him as a 'good Joe.' Now if you'll get off this phone so I can catch up on a little sleep, I'll slave some more for you tomorrow."

"You're holding out on me," Mr. Potter said quietly.

"What's that? Second sight?" Weston sounded disconcerted. "Oh, well. Did O'Toole tell you anything personal about me?"

"Nothing but what I told you."

"I thought perhaps he might have given you my background; he knows all about it. Fact is, I have a kind of bee in my bonnet. The reason I took you up on this job was because of the way Stendel's physician was killed."

"The physician! All right, you have astonished me. Now please elucidate."

"Car smashed. People killed. Children injured. That's what happened to me. A car smashed into mine. Drunken driver. Killed my wife and my two-year-old daughter and put me in the hospital for almost a year. That's when I was replaced in the D.A.'s office and ended as, and I quote, a private investigator."

It was the deadly quiet in the man's voice that disturbed Mr. Potter. "I didn't know," he said at last. "If I had—"

"You wouldn't have brought this particular job to me."

"Look here, Weston, I don't believe in preconceptions. No one knows why the doctor's brakes failed. No one knows whether that accident had anything to do with Stendel's murder—if Stendel was murdered. We haven't got a case, you know; we haven't even got a crime. So far.

29

Do you understand that?"

"If you mean will my personal experience warp my judgment," the detective replied, "I honestly don't know. All I can promise is that I'll try to keep an open mind. Look here, Potter, let's have an understanding right now. I'll follow every lead until it peters out. But if I find I'm getting one-sided, I'll tell you so. Fair enough?"

"Fair enough." Mr. Potter set down the telephone, dissatisfied. If he had known Weston's background, he'd have hesitated a long time before hiring him. It was easy enough to follow the direction the detective's thoughts were taking: from a wrecked car to a drunken driver to Burgess Holman.

There was nothing to be gained by worrying at this point. In any case, he'd see Burgess for himself. If he had already acquired an unsavory record, his father's alarm was understandable. Mr. Potter settled himself comfortably in bed and opened Maugham's *Of Human Bondage*. He realized now why he had selected it for the trip, a reminder that a man could lose his spiritual freedom and his judgment if he loved unwisely; a reminder of the woman who had died in Dr. Holman's sanitarium; a warning of the danger to his peace of mind that was implicit in Janet Grant.

After a moment he closed the book. Was it sheer coincidence that Winifred's second husband had been in Las Vegas as long as she had? Teddy Morris obviously had business there, but what was the attraction of a gambling town for Winifred Lawrence?

II

West of Chicago, Mr. Potter settled down on Route 66. As he drove farther southwest, the highways cleared, the sun came out, the car heater was switched off, and the windows were rolled down.

It was a lot of country, Mr. Potter thought, when he had clocked twenty-two hundred miles on the speedometer. A lot of empty country. A lot of sky. And not much water. In the Southwest one almost forgot the sound of rain.

High in a deep-blue sky a big bird seemed to hang motionless in the air, hovering over the emptiness below. "Like the shadow of a buzzard hovering over a man dying of thirst on the desert," Graham Collinge had said. Jokingly, of course. At the moment, it did not seem riotously funny, not the image any man would care to create. Because he distrusted introspection, Mr. Potter forced his mind back to the scenery. If emptiness could be called scenery. A lot of land.

A small pickup truck rattled past, driven by an Indian. Squatting on the floor in back was a woman in a cotton dress with two small boys who returned Mr. Potter's wave, staring at him with bright black eyes.

It was growing late when he braked his car, smiling in delighted amusement. Ahead of him a lazy horse pulled a surrey with a fringed top. The driver was a bearded man decked out with a frayed old straw hat, a gaudy plaid shirt tucked into blue jeans. Beside him sat a woman in a long, ruffled dress, her head covered by a sunbonnet. They belonged to the past century. He saw the sign on the side of the surrey, COME AND GIT IT AT THE CHUCK WAGON, and his smile faded. Advertising. He might have known. Thank God, no one could vulgarize Grand Canyon. Then he saw the motel and laughed aloud. Each unit was a replica of an Indian tepee but the sign read: ALL UNITS WITH FREE TELEVISION. The worst of two worlds, he decided.

He pulled up at the office behind a small car, from which its owner, emerging with a key, came up to him, grinning.

"Didja ever see anything to top this? Wish I could get some pictures but the light is wrong." Mr. Potter saw that he had a camera hung on a leather strap around his neck under a short car coat. "I'll get some in the morning, though. This is the kind of thing I've been looking for, You come down from the North Rim? Utah?"

Mr. Potter shook his head. "New York by way of Chicago."

"It's like another world up there. The ponderosa pines and the quaking aspens. The Indians on the Navajo Reservation and the herd of buffaloes on the plains. Thought at first cattle grew large out here. And the marble canyon! Couldn't believe it was real at first. Beauty like that." He made a hopeless gesture, unable to express the wonder that had widened his eyes.

Mr. Potter was reminded of Bottom trying in vain to translate into words the substance of his enchanted dream:

"I have had a dream, past the wit of man to say what dream it was. . . . Methought I was—there is no man can tell what. Methought I was—and methought I had—but man is but a patched fool, if he will offer to say what me-thought I had. The eye of man hath not heard, the ear of man hath not seen, man's hand is not able to taste, his tongue to conceive, nor his heart to report, what my dream was."

He was a stocky fellow with dark hair, a snub nose, and the voice of a frog. He realized belatedly that he was blocking the way. "I'll move my car. See you around." He came closer, peered at Mr. Potter. "Say, I know you. One thing I can say for myself, I never forget a face. I've got some pictures of you. Why, I've got a scrapbook right in the car. You'll be interested. Let's find some place and eat together tonight. My name is Ponders. Noah Ponders." He spoke modestly, as though he had presented Mr. Potter with a not-unworthy gift.

"But why me?" Mr. Potter said plaintively. "I mean why pictures of me?"

"I'm Noah Ponders," the other repeated, as though that ought to explain everything. "I get pix for the big magazines. I do books of photographs. I travel around the world and—"

"I know. You take pictures."

"That's it." Noah sounded happy that he had established a reasonable understanding. In fact, Noah was a happy man. "Usually I concentrate on celebrities, but now and then I put in other people, with their names, of course. They like it. They buy books."

"I won't." Mr. Potter was firm.

"Didn't expect you to." Noah was not in the least offended. "The others are sidelines, bread and butter. Now I'm doing what I've dreamed of all my life, a real social history of America. One picture is worth a thousand words. You ever hear that before? And is it true! Now take this stuff I've got on you."

"I'd like to. What do you want for it?"

There was no ruffling the essential sweetness of Noah's nature. "I wouldn't part with it! I've got a special section, you know. Every topic is in a section of its own: public events, politics, national disasters, society, celebrities, great natural wonders like Niagara Falls. You come under crime, of course."

There was no point in being annoyed. Mr. Potter burst out laughing and went into the office to engage a motel unit for the night and to ask about plane schedules for Las Vegas. He wasn't particularly surprised to find the camera

33

man hovering near his preposterous tepee when he came out to look for a restaurant. He had already foreseen that he was in for a long, long evening with Noah.

At first there was a struggle for position as Noah prodded in a determined way—he had apparently learned to be insensitive to snubs—to obtain personal information from Mr. Potter. Noah simply did not understand the meaning of privacy. If people were famous, they had their pictures taken, they answered questions about themselves. If they were news, they were public property and had no legitimate grievance.

This point Mr. Potter settled with a degree of firmness that made Noah blink. But though he lamented it, though he regarded his new acquaintance's attitude as a form of deplorable eccentricity, Noah accepted it amiably enough. On the whole, once he had been steered away from any discussion of the crimes in which Mr. Potter had been involved or any attempt to get an inside story about the people who had been concerned—and he was positively gluttonous for personal details—Mr. Potter rather enjoyed him. Though his enthusiasms were as indiscriminating as a child's, they were genuine; he was discovering his own country with an excitement that was rather touching. If it hadn't been for that hoarse and tireless voice, for Noah's passion for laboring the obvious, he might have been a pleasant companion.

But by ten o'clock the dose was enough and Mr. Potter firmly said good night, congratulating himself that, though he had looked at dozens of pictures of people who were "news," he had escaped having to look at any of himself. Wearily he set the alarm, hoping to be off before Noah was awake, as the latter had confided that he was going to develop some films before he went to bed.

Mr. Potter made his regular call, belatedly aware of the growing discrepancy in time from night to night. It must be after one in New York.

Weston answered sleepily. "Hell, you know what time it is here?"

"Sorry. I'll make it earlier after this."

Weston grunted. "Wait until I get my notes and a cigarette. Okay. Winifred's prince was duly divorced by her in Reno in 1933. He died nine or ten years ago in Brazil. You can include him out of the picture. Morris, the second husband, has been in Las Vegas for six weeks. He arrived at approximately the same time as Winifred and her party. He's staying at a moderately priced motel in the town. Winifred, her fourth husband, and the two young men, her son and her nephew, are on the Strip, very gaudy place, high-class entertainment. If Winifred and Morris have met, there's no rumor of it. Still, as you know yourself, milling around the tables from place to place, as people do, nothing could be easier than a surreptitious exchange of some sort.

"Bertha Christie, the nurse, left by plane from New York several days ago and made a stopover to visit an old friend. She'll be in Flagstaff tomorrow. I got that from Dr. Holman's office. And, by the way, he was greatly relieved to know you are on the job."

"Anything else?"

"Burgess Holman went out to San Francisco to visit his grandfather some time in the late fall. The general impression is that he wanted money. In fact, he always wants money. Stendel read his new will aloud a week after the grandson arrived. Burgess stayed on there after Stendel's death and he is still with the Las Vegas party. That's the budget for today. For God's sake, next time you call, remember the time difference. Three hours, for God's sake!"

"You're holding out again."

"Oh."

"Well?"

Weston sounded oddly uncertain. "I'm not laboring this, Potter, but I tracked down a guy I used to know on the San Francisco *Chronicle*. He gets around. Stendel's physician was a Dr. Mourner—hell of a name for a general practitioner, isn't it? His car had just been serviced and nothing was wrong with the brakes. For those hills, they check and double-check. My friend found the garage that took care of the doc's car, which was too badly damaged for repair and resale so it had been towed to a junk yard. My friend got hold of an expert mechanic and they went out to inspect it."

"Well?" Mr. Potter broke the tantalizing silence.

Weston's voice rose in excitement. "There had been a fire in the junk yard. The cars were a mass of twisted metal."

"When did this happen?"

"Right after Mourner's car was turned in." When Mr. Potter made no comment Weston drawled, "I know. No proof. Call it coincidence. Call it accident. We have no case."

"Just don't develop any blind spots," Mr. Potter advised him.

"There were a couple of small children involved in that multiple crash in which Mourner and two other people were killed," Weston said softly. "One of those kids is going to be lame; the other one is minus a hand for life. Pretty, isn't it?"

"Damnable," Mr. Potter agreed. "But what do you plan to do, Weston? Spend the rest of your life tracking down

36

the people who cause automobile accidents?"

"I'd like to! By God, I'd like to!" Then the tension relaxed and Weston's tone was mocking. "Okay, Potter, that's the budget for today. That's the story so far. Wait for our next thrilling installment. How's the weather out there?"

"Warm and sunny."

In the morning, Mr. Potter shut off the alarm and dressed quickly, anxious to escape from Noah Ponders and his eternal camera, his eternal voice, his eternal platitudes. He dropped his suitcase in the car and did not slam the door until he had safely passed the motel. Here and there, as the sun rose higher, he caught a brief glimpse of fantastic color on the rough dunes.

By the time he reached Flagstaff, a small crowd had already gathered at the airport. There were a bus for the South Rim of Grand Canyon, a taxi, and half a dozen private cars. He heard a voice from a loudspeaker, a speck appeared in the sky and grew to a bird, then a plane circled and came down in a smooth landing. Mr. Potter parked his car hastily and walked toward the plane. He saw a stocky figure with dark hair and a camera hung around his neck under a short coat. O God, Noah again!

Then a woman's high-pitched voice called, "Christie! Christie! Here we are."

The stocky figure turned and Mr. Potter realized that it was a woman wearing dark slacks. He took half a step in her direction, saw the girl who moved with a distinction and grace that were all her own. The sun shone on fair hair and long dark eyes under tilted brows. He stopped short.

"Hello, Hiram," she said quietly.

"Janet!"

A car door slammed and a long Cadillac slid away from the airport. On the back seat, wedged between a man and a woman, Mr. Potter could see the nurse's clipped dark hair. As he watched, the car picked up speed.

4

"THAT," JANET GRANT said, "is Bertha Christie, the trained nurse in whom you are so interested. As I told you, Mrs. Lawrence sent for her because she is on the verge of a nervous breakdown. After showing Miss Christie Grand Canyon, the Lawrences are going to drive her to Las Vegas."

She looked at Mr. Potter but he had never, she recalled, had a revealing face. At the moment it seemed very remote. To a stranger it might appear ordinary, that of any man one passed on the street. Only when he was off-guard had she seen the implacability of which he was capable; the cool courage which he understated; and for one minute, one single minute, a depth of passion to which she had responded like a thirsty plant to water. Never again had he been off-guard, or perhaps that minute had been only a flash of summer lightning. I'll stay until I find out, she told herself.

She went on patiently, "Miss Christie seemed unhappy

about the trip and a bit on edge. She's worried about something. This was her first flight and that bothered her, too, so I offered to come along. It's a small thing to do for her after all her kindness to us; anyhow, I knew you were concerned about her and I thought I might as well see she got here all right. I owe you that."

She knew at once, by the tightening of his mouth, that she had made a tactical error but she would only emphasize her mistake if she attempted to retract it.

"I wish," he began, broke off. "You don't owe me anything, Janet. I wish you could believe that." He looked in the direction the Cadillac had taken, and said uneasily, "I shouldn't have let her go. I was caught off balance. I meant to keep an eye on her and then—my attention was distracted."

"You mustn't let that happen again," she told him gently.

He started to answer her, decided, for reasons that he did not care to analyze, to let it go. "Is anyone meeting you?"

"There should be a bus around somewhere for the South Rim."

"You're going to Grand Canyon, too! Then let me run you up. It's not over eighty miles. My car's right here." He was aware that his voice revealed too much exhilaration for the role he had set himself but it seemed to be beyond his control. When he had piled her suitcases into the trunk of the car he asked, "Have you had lunch?"

"On the plane. It's hard to realize that New York City is only hours away by air." When he made no comment she gave him a sidelong look and spoke while her courage was high. "There's a Chinese tradition that we owe our lives to people who save them. Payment on demand, Hiram." At least she had made herself clear. From now on she'd have to leave it up to him. Somewhat to her own surprise she was not embarrassed.

For twenty miles, thirty, forty, they drove in silence, at a slow, almost absentminded pace. There was plenty of time.

"Deer," he said at length, and she turned as three deer silently merged into the background, though there seemed no place for them to merge among the widely spaced, regal ponderosa pines with their dark red trunks.

"What a pity," she said at last, "that people haven't the dignity of trees."

She was intent on the landscape now and he risked a quick look at her. He had quite definitely made up his mind never to see her again. Now that she sat so quietly beside him, so undemandingly, it seemed like a drastic idea. But she had come to offer him her gratitude. "Payment on demand." He didn't want her that way. But it would be easier to establish a firm position, he thought, if she weren't so distractingly pretty.

When he spoke he tried to conceal any uneasiness he might feel. "I hope that nurse, Miss Christie, isn't telling the Lawrences that you came out here to keep an eye on her."

"She won't," Janet said without hesitation.

"Sure about that?"

"I never even suggested that I was coming on her account, Hiram. I said I was planning to go to Grand Canyon and why not make the flight together."

"And no one will wonder why you just happened to come at this off-season?"

"Oh, I explained that," she assured him.

"Look here, Janet, this is a queer situation. I'd rather not have you involved."

"I'm not going to interfere; you may be sure of that."

When he made no reply she said, "Tell me whatever you like. Nothing that you don't want to."

And in the long run he told her the whole story. She thought about it, taking her time. "What a ghastly situation! Then Miss Christie could be in danger, couldn't she? Hiram, you've got to stop it. She's really a very fine person."

"I'll do my best. The problem is that I can't declare myself and if any of them find out about my past activities it will put the lid on or—hasten things."

There was amused affection in her look. "You never quite realize, do you, that most people know something about your past activities. You're by way of being a celebrity. When your friends get in a jam they have a habit of turning to you, hoping you'll find some way of extricating them." There was the shadow of a smile on her lips which he did not see. "Of course, your trip to Grand Canyon could have a perfectly innocent explanation, like mine."

"One thing strikes me," he said slowly. "You were shocked at the idea that Miss Christie might be in danger; you weren't really shocked at the idea that one of the Lawrence party might be dangerous."

"That's queer," she exclaimed. "I hadn't realized it myself. I don't mean I'd ever have thought of it but I don't have the slightest impulse to say, 'No! They couldn't have killed old Jake Stendel. None of them could hurt Miss Christie.' "

"How well do you know these people, Janet?"

"As I told you over the telephone, I haven't seen any of them in four years. I don't know what they are like now. I've known the boys for years. We're about the same age and we moved in pretty much the same circles. And when I came out, they went to most of the parties."

42

"Do you like them?"

"Well—" She considered the question. "Damon is awfully attractive but he's got an odd sort of nature. Charming to outsiders but simply beastly to his mother in a nasty-nice, mocking sort of way. Sometimes I think he really hates her. As for Burgess Holman, his cousin, no one could possibly like him. A vain, arrogant, dominating creature. Dominating with nothing to dominate with."

Mr. Potter laughed. "That's quite a trick."

"He looks like his grandfather, old Jake Stendel, but he couldn't be more different. Jake was a fighter; Burgess is a whiner. He's like a battered prizefighter who never won a prize. He gets drunk and he's offensive at parties. As a rule he begins to tell everyone how great a composer he is."

"How do the two cousins get along?"

"I don't know how things are now. I used to meet them both at a lot of parties but never together. You can hardly think of them together; they're so wildly unlike, except for their voices, of course. Can't tell one from the other."

"What about Winifred Lawrence?"

"It's hard for me to be fair. When Dad's will was made public after Cass was arrested, and people learned that I had been put on a small allowance, Mrs. Lawrence was really vicious. She made sure I understood that she would do everything in her power to prevent me from marrying Damon, that she would never accept me."

"Did that matter so much?"

"You mean on account of Damon? Oh, no. It was just one more humiliation."

"At least you have your own money now."

Janet was amused. "It will be interesting to see how she reacts, won't it? To make a fuss over me now would be so blatant she would hardly dare try."

The road began to climb. Already the light was fading from the sky. "Look to your right," he told her and heard a sharp, indrawn breath.

After a long time Janet said in a shaken voice, "The pictures don't really tell the story, do they? I thought the canyon was just a view."

They did not speak again until Mr. Potter pulled into the parking lot at the hotel where there were only a few cars, not surprising so early in the season. One of them, he saw in relief, was the Cadillac that had taken Miss Christie away from the airport. There was a second car with a California license plate, a rakish little red MG with a muddy paper streamer wrapped around a wheel, the kind that appears with signs reading, JUST MARRIED. Mr. Potter looked at it thoughtfully.

"We'll get the luggage later. Are you warm enough?"

Now that the sun was sinking, there was an icy bite in the air. Janet fastened the collar of her coat, pulled up the hood over her hair, let him lead her out to the rim. Already the vast abyss was in darkness. Here and there, purple shadows touched the sides of the canyon. Near the rim the setting sun picked out small mounds that were mountains, a little niche in which the Eiffel Tower could have nestled. Then the sun dropped like a plummet.

"Who was it," her voice was shaken, "who said an astronomer had to be inoculated against eternity? That's the way this makes me feel."

They went into the hotel lobby where a tree trunk blazed and crackled in a mammoth fireplace.

"I am Janet Grant," she said to the desk clerk. "I have a reservation."

"Miss Grant? We expected you earlier by the airport bus. You were the only passenger they had to pick up."

44

There was a hint of reproach in the clerk's voice.

"I met a friend who was kind enough to give me a lift."

While Mr. Potter signed the register, the clerk looked from one face to the other with a discreet and understanding smirk that made Mr. Potter long to kick his backside. Janet seemed unaware of it.

"How about having a drink with me in half an hour?" he suggested.

"That's definitely an idea."

When she had gone to her room he stood in the lobby staring at the great fire. There was no sign of Christie or of the couple who had removed her so expeditiously from the airport. Only one other person shared the lobby with him, a man who sat before the fire on a bench that was covered with an Indian blanket. Dark glasses failed to conceal the scars on his cheekbones. His left hand was badly twisted. In his right he held a heavy stick with a curved handle. Passive as his face and body were, the right hand seemed to live a restless life of its own, beating out on the wooden handle a constantly repeated rhythm (− . . − −).

A quarter of an hour later, an interval during which Mr. Potter patiently read brochures on the mule trail, the sightseeing trips, and a geological survey of the canyon, a bus panted to a stop and members of a conducted tour trooped in, a trifle self-conscious but determined to make sure they were getting everything that had been guaranteed by their all-expense trip. The driver stacked luggage in a great pile and the clerk was occupied with registrations and a barrage of questions.

Once more the door opened and Mr. Potter's heart sank. He should have expected it! There stood Noah Ponders, beaming at Mr. Potter, at the great fire, at his general good fortune in being alive and in this delightful place. You couldn't dislike Noah. You simply tried to avoid him.

"Well," he said inevitably, pumping Mr. Potter's hand as though he had finally tracked down Dr. Livingstone, "it's a small world."

"Christie," cried a high voice, "I couldn't imagine where you were. Oh"—as Noah turned around—"I thought you were someone else."

Winifred Lawrence was about fifty-five, a thin, haggard woman with dyed brown hair, haunted eyes, and a heavily made-up, discontented mouth. Everything that clothes could do for her had been done, but it wasn't enough. The shrill voice, the burning eyes, the tense throat cords indicated that she had not exaggerated in saying that her nerves were shot to pieces. She was accompanied by an extremely good-looking young man in his twenties who seemed familiar until Mr. Potter realized that he bore a startling resemblance to the wedding picture of the handsome actor, Damon Knox.

Winifred said fretfully, "Damon, do try to find Christie, will you? I'm simply perishing for a cocktail."

"I told you before," he said in a lazy voice, "that she went out with your Fourth to look at the canyon."

"Please!" Winifred's voice was edged with irritation. "You know how I hate having you speak of James like that. Anyhow, it's absurd. Christie can't see anything in the dark and it's beastly cold."

A young couple came in, the girl with her hair more disarranged than the wind would explain, her companion with a heavy smear of lipstick on his cheek; obviously the honeymoon couple from the red MG. Another couple followed them.

"Oh, here they are!" There was so much relief in Winifred's voice that Mr. Potter realized she had been genuinely afraid. What had she imagined might happen to Christie? Or what did she suppose Christie and James Lawrence had been discussing?

The sturdy woman from the plane was accompanied by a plump, ruddy-faced man who could hardly be more than thirty-five.

"Man, that fire looks good! Glad you're down, darling. We need a hot toddy. I wonder if that bartender remembers how to make one." He rubbed his hands together. A good Joe. The dependable type. The man who makes the party move but keeps it under control.

"What on earth made you go out in the dark, James?" Winifred asked petulantly. "And it's chilly when the sun goes down. You know how susceptible you are to colds."

"Don't worry about me, darling. I was all wrapped up."

"It was my fault," Christie explained. "I couldn't wait for my first real look at the canyon and Mr. Lawrence was good enough to go with me."

"But you can't see a thing now!"

"So I discovered." Bertha Christie was a plump woman of about Winifred's age, with only a few strands of gray in her short dark hair. Her face was round, her skin smooth, she had a turned-up nose and observant eyes. Without any attempt to make herself attractive, she appeared younger than her patient. Her matter-of-fact voice and manner seemed to provide a steadying factor.

"I'll get rid of my coat and be right down. Don't wait for me."

"You take it, Damon," Lawrence suggested. "Save the gal a trip. I'll stir up the bartender."

He could hardly be more than eight years older than his stepson but he handled the difficult problem of their relationship with exceptional tact, steering an even course between the attitude of a contemporary and that of the man of authority. It was, Mr. Potter thought, very well done.

"That's an idea," the younger man said cheerfully. He took the coat, turned, and a slow smile crept over his attractive face as Janet came into the lobby, wearing a deceptively simple dress of crimson wool.

"Janet! This is my lucky day." He took her hand, leaned forward to kiss her cheek. "Mother, you remember Janet Grant, of course. Come over here by the fire. Mother's Present Incumbent is getting us all some hot rum punch."

"Hello, Damon." She smiled at Winifred. "Sorry, not this time. I'm having a drink with Hiram Potter. Do you know each other?"

She made the introductions while Mr. Potter thought that this was an unexpected dividend. Janet was smoothing the way for him. What he had not taken into consideration was Noah Ponders. The latter, as adept as a politician in search of votes at shoving his way through a crowd to get in the foreground, pushed past the new arrivals to Janet.

"Miss Grant!" Her look of surprise did not daunt him. "Isn't this pleasant! So many celebrities in one place. I've got pictures of you taken at your brother's murder trial."

Janet's face was quite expressionless. She looked at him without speaking.

"To think of meeting you here! And Mrs. Lawrence, too. Why I have pictures of you going back for years."

There was a small smile on Damon's handsome mouth.

"And Mr. Potter! He," Noah explained exuberantly to anyone within earshot, "is simply fabulous. He's the man who really solved the Fatal Lady Case and cleared Cass Grant. He—"

Janet took one look at Mr. Potter's dismayed expression and moved to stand beside him, her hand on his arm.

48

"Hiram Potter," she said firmly, "has gone out of circulation. Once and for all."

The smile faded from Damon's face. Winifred said, "I congratulate you, Mr. Potter. Janet is a lovely girl." She added, as though defending her opinion against dissenters, "I always said so, no matter what anyone thought. And it's so nice to know that she's got back her share of the Grant money."

That woman, Mr. Potter thought, is pure poison. Vindictive, but in such a stupid way. He glanced at Janet. Her long eyes studied the older woman rather mercilessly.

"Thank heavens, Hiram is so disgustingly rich that he needn't be concerned about money. That's one problem I don't have to bother about."

Winifred looked at her, uncertain of her meaning. "When is it to be?"

"Later in the spring. But there has been so much publicity," and she gave Noah what she hoped was a quelling look, "that Hiram and I decided to get away for a while. Cass expected to come with us but he was delayed at the last moment. Ever since his release, that brother of mine has plunged into all sorts of unexpected enterprises, making up for lost time. He'll join us any day, I suppose."

"Well," Lawrence said heartily, "it looks as though we drink a toast." He took the napkin-wrapped glasses from the waiter's tray and distributed them. "To you both. And great happiness."

"Thank you." There was a twinkle in Mr. Potter's eyes as he looked at Janet. She raised her glass and smiled at him over the rim.

"So this," Christie said in her comfortable voice, "is your young man."

Lawrence laughed. "Trust Christie to be the first to

49

know."

"We had lots of time on the plane," the nurse explained, "and—you know how it is—we exchanged confidences."

There was a curious hush, then the sound of a caught breath. Mr. Potter's face set. That settled the matter. Janet would be shipped back to New York if he had to send her in protective custody.

The members of the conducted tour had been shepherded to their rooms, the lobby was deserted except for the small group that was stationed around the big fire. Noah Ponders had managed to insinuate himself into their midst, probably in preparation for a section of his book of Americana to be called "Celebrities I Have Met." The only person who remained aloof was the crippled man who was staring into the fire as though unaware of their presence.

Noah looked around him, so filled with goodwill that it reached out to all of them, even the lame man who remained outside the charmed circle. "Now isn't this pleasant." He leaned forward, half smiling, half frowning. "I know you. I'm sure I know you. Only I just can't call your name to mind."

The lame man turned his head briefly to glance at him. "Your mistake." There was no annoyance in his voice; he simply dismissed Noah and returned to his thoughts.

"Sometimes it's like that," Noah agreed amiably. "You see someone out of context and you can't place him. Like —well, you see your milkman at the football game, or an actor buying a pair of shoes, or your druggist at the theater. You know—out of context. I know you all right. Never forget a face."

As the man's face was hideously scarred, Mr. Potter regarded this as one of Noah's more unfortunate statements.

The lame man, however, seemed to have forgotten him. He sat motionless as before, only his right hand continuing its tireless, incessant beat on the handle of his stick.

"I've got a picture of you, too," Noah said to Damon. "Taken—well—uh—a picture." His voice dwindled away uncertainly.

It must, Mr. Potter thought, be quite a picture to cause Noah the thick-skinned any social embarrassment.

Damon made a sudden movement that upset his glass and the scalding rum splashed on his leg. "Damn, I'll have to change." He set down the glass, which rattled as he put it on the table before the fire.

That boy's sick, Mr. Potter thought, and took a step in his direction. No, he's had a shock. Damon went quickly out of the lobby. Mr. Potter saw him pause to steady himself momentarily against the wall and then he was gone like a man in flight. Only Christie showed any awareness of his condition; and she looked after him, her soft, good-humored mouth tightening.

"Burgess!" Winifred waved her hand and a stocky young man with a heavy face, heavy eyebrows, heavy lips, and the cumbersome movements of a bear joined them.

"Hi, Christie!" He bent to kiss her. "All Aunt Winifred has to do is send out an SOS and you come running."

"You know Christie's motto." Lawrence smiled at the nurse. "Never fail a Stendel."

"Well, hardly ever," Burgess drawled. Different as the cousins were, they had the same lazy, mocking voices. "Janet! How wonderful." He lumbered toward her, tried to take her in his arms.

Oaf, Mr. Potter found himself thinking in fury. Take your hands off her.

Janet held him away, laughing. "What exuberance,

Burgess."

"She's bespoke, boy," Lawrence told him. "Here's the lucky guy. Mr. Potter, my wife's nephew, Burgess Holman."

"So that's what shook Damon," Burgess said in a tone of satisfaction. "He went past me in the hall looking as though someone had landed him a poke in the solar plexus."

"Don't be silly." Winifred's voice was sharp. "He just spilled his drink. He got over Janet years ago."

"As a matter of fact," Burgess said coolly, "neither of us has ever got over her."

In a few minutes Damon returned. He had changed to dark slacks and there was no trace of emotion on his good-looking face.

"You've heard the bad news?" Burgess indicated Janet and Mr. Potter.

Damon grinned maliciously. "What did you expect her to do? Wait for your opera to be produced?"

"Or for you to break into show business?" Burgess retorted.

Both Janet and Lawrence plunged into the breach, starting to speak at the same time, and Damon turned to Christie with a shrug. She was watching him with thoughtful, worried eyes. Mr. Potter suspected that she was deeply fond of the boy but that, for some reason, she was unable to trust him.

Burgess tossed a heavy log into the fireplace with such violence that a shower of sparks flew out, touching the lame man's trouser legs. Before Mr. Potter could move, Damon brushed them off with a muttered apology.

A late traveler came into the lobby, a slim, elegant man in his fifties, and went to the desk. As the clerk pushed forward the registration card, the newcomer made a swift appraising survey of the room and its occupants. A successful industrialist who had retired early, Mr. Potter thought. Then he changed his mind. If it weren't that national parks and resorts whose chief attractions are scenery and outdoor sports were not fruitful ground for such people, he'd be inclined to set this one down as a high-powered confidence man. Perhaps it was because he was too much the Man of Distinction to be anything but a photographer's model; perhaps it was the expression of limpid honesty where one would have expected shrewd intelligence.

And then, for the second time that evening, Damon overturned his glass. "Good God! There's mother's Second!"

5

Even with the members of the conducted tour, the big dining room seemed almost empty. Mr. Potter had selected a table for two at some distance from the others and now he sat facing Janet, his back to the room.

"I hope it hasn't caused you any trouble," she said anxiously, "but I knew you didn't want anyone to guess why you were really here, and after that man Ponders rushed in to broadcast the bad tidings, I thought something ought to be done."

"Noah and his bark! In a way it was inevitable. I suppose I should have been prepared. At least you behaved nobly."

"You aren't angry?" She was watching him in a kind of alarm.

He began to laugh. "If we're going to get away with this, you mustn't look as though you were on the verge of tears. You should give the impression that you find me devastatingly attractive."

"I'll take lessons from the honeymoon couple. They are so absorbed in each other they don't know what is going on around them. It must be wonderful to be so much in love."

Mr. Potter ordered cocktails and retired rather hastily behind his menu. When the frosty glasses had been set before them and they had given their orders he said, "We've got to have a little talk, you know. Right now we are sitting on a keg of dynamite."

"You mean the arrival of Mrs. Lawrence's second husband? Of all the fantastic coincidences!" She saw his expression. "Oh, you don't believe it was a coincidence, do you?"

"I can't. Morris didn't even pretend to be surprised. It was Winifred who was shaken right down to her shoes."

"I've never seen her look so awful." Janet was careful to keep her voice low, though no one was seated near them. "And the casual way he strolled over there and—sort of took charge!"

For a moment they were both silent, remembering the scene. Morris had raised his brows when he heard Damon's exclamation. Then he had gone to join them, his face alight with synthetic pleasure.

"Hello, Winifred! This is a delightful surprise. I wish you'd tell me the secret of your eternal youth." He seized the hand she had not offered him, looking into her ravaged face on which the rouge stood out against the pallor.

"Hello, Teddy. Are you staying here long?"

"No idea," he said cheerfully. "I'll just see what the place has to offer. Well, Burgess." His eyes rested for a moment on the highball glass. Burgess had rejected the hot rum punch with a brief but eloquent expletive. "Still lifting them, I see. How are you, Damon boy? I've been watching the theatrical columns for news of you. Takes a lot of perseverance to get started, doesn't it?" He added thoughtfully, "And talent, of course." He took both Christie's hands in his. "And good old Christie! Always sticking by the family."

He had gone through the group like a blockbuster, apparently unaware that, aside from Winifred's choked words, no one had spoken. He smiled at Lawrence and held out his hand. "You'll be James Lawrence. I'm Theodore Morris." He chuckled. "Your predecessor. One of them, at least. It's always fascinating, I think, to meet a successor. You get such interesting sidelights."

For a moment it had appeared to the spectators of this domestic comedy that it was going to turn into melodrama. Winifred was on the verge of a first-class scene. Then she controlled herself with an effort that left her shaking.

For once, Lawrence seemed to be out of his depth. He accepted Morris's hand, held it as though he didn't know what to do with it, and then released it as quickly as possible. He muttered, "How do you do," and then gathered his forces. "Ready for dinner, darling?" He looked around his small party, excluded Morris with an unenthusiastic, "Be seeing you around, I suppose," and herded them ahead of him into the dining room like a solicitous shepherd.

"What are they doing now?" Mr. Potter asked Janet.

"That man Morris is sitting by himself at a table against the wall, keeping an eye on everyone. Oh, dear God! Noah Ponders just barged in and asked if he could join him."

Mr. Potter smiled reassuringly. "Noah probably scents a story for his section on society, which he will spell with a capital S. Don't look so appalled; I doubt if Morris misses much. In any case, Noah can't do me any more harm than has been done already."

"I can't imagine a lovelier way of putting it," Janet told him.

He looked at her aghast. "Good heavens, I didn't mean that!"

She laughed at his chagrin. "You hadn't expected this sort of complication, had you?" For fear he would mistake her meaning she added hastily, "Morris putting in an appearance."

"Well, not here, certainly, though I was more or less prepared to have him on the scene at Las Vegas."

"What do you think he is up to? I can't see the point of all this."

"For one thing, he is breaking Winifred's nerve. That little episode before dinner was a declaration of war, if I ever saw one."

He broke off as the manager stopped at their table. "Everything satisfactory?" When he had been reassured, he placed paper and pens before them. "We like to feel that our guests here are our friends. The personal touch. We ask each of them to write some comment for us, just a sentence or two. I hope you'll oblige us." He went on to the next table.

Mr. Potter grinned at his companion. "A painless operation," he assured her and scrawled a few words.

"Oh, well." Janet, resigned, followed suit. "There's one thing that puzzles me."

"Only one? How fortunate you are."

"Damon and Burgess really hate each other. They never miss a chance to put in a barb where it will hurt most. Then why does Burgess hang around?"

"The irresistible appeal of the Stendel money, I'd think. By the way, what do these people live on while they are waiting for the estate to be settled?"

"I don't really know. I'm pretty sure Winifred has always had an allowance from her father but nothing excessive. Her husband—husbands—were expected to support themselves. One of old Jake's theories."

"And the boys?"

"He said they should become self-supporting and amount to something on their own. Follow his example. I don't know, Hiram. I imagine Winifred gives Damon something and, so far as I know, he's really tried hard to break into the theater. As for Burgess—if you know Dr. Holman, you can guess he told his son it was time he went out on his own. Burgess wouldn't like that. I rather expect he's living on Winifred as long as he can get away with it."

She was deep in thought, barely noticing what she ate. "Damon was certainly stunned when he saw Morris at the desk. You remember how he upset his glass?"

"For the second time. But what startled him the first time? He's not a clumsy man; far from it. He has all the disciplined grace of a good actor. Was it your announcement of our engagement?"

Janet shook her head. "Definitely not. I saw quite a bit of him, perhaps a dozen dates, before Cass was arrested. That's all. He's too vain to fall hard for any girl unless she simply swoons with admiration."

"And Burgess?"

"He tried to date me, but it was largely because Damon did. At least, that was my impression. Burgess has always been jealous of Damon because he's so good-looking and popular. Queer, isn't it, that the pretty woman had the ugly son. Heredity plays strange tricks. Anyhow, Burgess wasn't really interested in me."

"He seemed to be, tonight."

"That," Janet said tartly, "was the irresistible appeal of

the Grant money."

"But he's got a fortune coming to him." After a pause, Mr. Potter said thoughtfully, "Or perhaps he has a suspicion he'll find himself way out on a limb. Would you say he's a spendthrift?"

"Not especially. The chief reason he wants money is to help him get his opera produced."

"What kind of opera?" Mr. Potter asked idly.

"Oscar Wilde's *Portrait of Dorian Gray* done with masks like O'Neill, recurrent themes like Wagner, and what he calls a passionate dissonance that is all his own."

"Good God!" Mr. Potter ejaculated weakly.

"And," she continued, warming to her task, "it has Freudian overtones not only in the libretto but in the harmonic structure."

"You're making this up, you wretched girl."

"And that's not the worst."

"I'm not going to believe another word."

"This opera is his first work. He's never done any composing at all before. He told me so." She looked at Mr. Potter who was beyond speech. "He went to one of the great composers, I can't remember which, and asked for assistance with his opera. The composer suggested that he begin in a smaller way, writing songs, and Burgess was furious. So the composer told him the story about Mozart. You know the one. A young man went to ask him how to write a symphony and Mozart suggested that he start with a quartet. The young man said, 'But you started with symphonies.' 'Yes,' Mozart answered, 'but I didn't have to ask how.' "

Mr. Potter abandoned the subject of the opera to protect his tottering reason. "You know there could be another explanation for Damon being so upset. The picture

59

Ponders took of him and then was so coy about. Damon didn't like the idea a bit. That clause in Stendel's will has all three of them in a fever."

Janet's eyes widened and she looked carefully down at her plate.

"What's wrong?"

"The poor man who was sitting by the fire. He's just come in. I hadn't realized he was so horribly crippled, so disfigured."

He saw that she was genuinely shocked and he distracted her attention quickly. "Janet, has anything struck you about the nurse?"

She nodded. "Everyone, except Burgess, keeps hammering away at the point that she is so loyal to the family. You know, Hiram, I used to talk to her when she nursed my father. Not a lot, but you get a picture of a person. I don't believe she would let personal loyalty stand in the way of professional integrity, no matter how fond she was of anyone."

"But she already has," he reminded her. "She did when she broke the glass with the traces of white arsenic in it. And she's not really fond of these people. Grateful, perhaps, but there's no personal affection, except for Damon. She is worried about the boy but she doesn't quite know what to make of him."

"Hiram," her voice was hardly above a whisper, "did Mrs. Lawrence kill her father?"

"I don't know," he said heavily, "but Morris has some lever, a strangle hold. She's afraid of him. Look here, you've been a tremendous help. Will you do one thing more for me?"

"Yes," she said without hesitation.

"Send yourself a telegram and go back to New York.

60

This situation is explosive and I don't want you around when it blows up. You might get hurt."

It was some time before she answered. "If I go back now, what plausible reason will you have for staying on and especially for trailing along to Las Vegas? Noah Ponders is probably retailing your whole career right now to Morris. The wealthy Mr. Potter, the catalyst who gets involved in murder and makes things happen. If there is anything really wrong here, these people will all be wary of you. No, Hiram, I'm going to stay. I know the boys better than you possibly can; I could find out more about them, at least."

"I won't have you involved."

"I've already involved myself." She broke off as the manager passed their table, deftly retrieving the statements he had extorted from them.

There was a flash of light. Someone tittered. A woman exclaimed, "Oh, and my hair looks just awful!"

"It's Noah Ponders," Janet explained. "He is taking pictures of the tour group and getting their names and addresses. They love it."

"This," Mr. Potter said firmly, "is where we clear out. Your brother is going to hit the roof if he sees a picture of you taken with an unheralded fiancé, particularly if anything should happen."

"But Cass knows—"

"Have you finished?"

She looked at him and then got up without a word. As they started toward the door they saw Noah snap Morris's picture while the latter looked smilingly at the camera; then the photographer turned to the bride and groom, who looked smilingly at each other. He advanced toward the crippled man who sat alone and who had removed his dark glasses while he studied the menu. Puckered white scars ran across his cheekbones and lifted a corner of his mouth. As Noah raised his camera, the man flung up his good hand, partly in protest, partly to shield his mutilated face.

There was a flash and Noah moved on toward the Lawrence table. Damon knocked over his chair as he leaped, swinging at Noah, sending him backward at a staggering run.

"Damon," his mother cried shrilly, "are you crazy?"

"Steady on there, boy," Lawrence protested.

Damon continued to advance on Noah who had regained his balance and was gaping at his assailant in bewilderment. "What's the idea?" he demanded, not in anger but in the tone of a much-injured man.

"We don't want our pictures taken. When people don't want their pictures taken, let them alone!" Damon said savagely.

Noah strove to be reasonable. "Look here, this is the way I earn my living."

"Then starve, for all I care. But if I see that camera around again, you bastard, I'll smash it."

"Speaking of bastards," Morris said.

Damon swung toward him but Morris did not move. For a moment the two men stared at each other and then Morris said, his voice unstressed, "Let the guy alone."

Damon straightened his tie, turned around and went out of the dining room. With an air of defiance that made him seem very young he whistled softly to himself.

Lawrence looked at Mr. Potter and Janet who were passing his table. He got up, shaking his head ruefully. "I guess that was just the artistic temperament. I'm a plain businessman myself so I'm out of my depth."

"After all," Burgess said lazily, "there must be some way in which Damon can display his artistic temperament."

"You ought to know," Winifred snapped. "I haven't seen your name in lights anywhere."

"Not even in headlines," he admitted. "Oh, well, early days yet."

The nurse appeared to be exhausted by the family squabbles. "Will you excuse me?" she said abruptly. "If you don't need me tonight, Mrs. Knox—Mrs. Lawrence, I'd like to rest up from the trip. It was my first flight, you know, and quite an exciting experience, but tiring."

"You put yourself right to bed," Lawrence told her heartily. "You're on vacation. I'll look after my girl." He patted Winifred's hand. There was sheer adoration in the look she gave him.

While the members of the tour group were besieging the clerk with questions about the next day's excursion down the mule trail, Mr. Potter drifted behind the desk to help himself to a map. Hastily he looked at the registration cards. The members of the tour he set aside. Apart from the Lawrence party, that left only Noah Ponders (Washington, D.C.), Theodore Morris (Las Vegas), Mr. and Mrs. John Smith (San Francisco), and Albert Munn (San Francisco).

Thoughtfully he put the cards back, drew from the scattered testimonials on the desk those written by the people who interested him, and went to join Janet and a still-smoldering Damon before the fire. In a few moments the crippled man made his way painfully out of the dining room.

Damon got up. "I've taken your place, sir, I'm afraid."

"I don't own it. Anyhow, I'm on my way to bed." Munn smiled. "But thank you."

63

By nine-thirty the lobby was almost deserted as the members of the conducted tour were preparing to rise early and the Lawrence party had gone upstairs. Noah, still aggrieved, went off after examining his camera anxiously to make sure it had not been damaged.

Janet yawned. "It may be only nine-thirty here but it's twelve-thirty by my personal clock and I was up at five. Good night, Hiram."

Morris, who had been nursing a drink, wandered over to join Mr. Potter by the fire, apparently in a mood for confidences. "There's a lot to be said for being childless. Those two young jerks are the best reasons I can think of, Winifred's boy and Helen's. You knew I was married once to Winifred Lawrence?"

"You made that fairly clear before dinner."

Morris looked quickly at Mr. Potter. "Very friendly. No hard feelings. When she met Knox it was all up with me. I could have told her that it wouldn't last but Winifred wants what she wants when she wants it. I wouldn't stand in her way so I took myself off. Cleared out of her life."

"Very sporting of you," Mr. Potter commented, his face and voice blank of expression.

"Well, what else can you do? No point in being a dog in the manger. And Winifred had it coming to her. Yes, you could almost feel sorry for the poor old girl. Helen had all the looks of the family and Winifred could never compete. But she tried. How she tried! She ran off with her prince, thinking she'd show up Helen when she had a title, but he was a no-good bum if there ever was one. When he found out he couldn't get his hands on any of the Stendel money, he walked out on her."

It was curious to see how the surface polish vanished when Morris talked. Silent, he appeared to be a distinguished man; when he spoke, the cracks in the veneer were obvious.

"Then, she married me but I didn't have the old razzle-dazzle of Knox. She took one look at him and went down for the count. They parted over in France and all that Winifred got out of that was Damon junior. Did you see how he went for that poor guy with the camera tonight? The bastard!"

Mr. Potter finished his cigarette. He wondered how much of the gambler's unsolicited confidence could be attributed to what Noah Ponders had undoubtedly said about his activities. All of it, probably. Morris wasn't a man to make a play without being sure where the cards lay. He wasn't a man, either, to carry the conversational ball alone. He was watching Mr. Potter in some perplexity. Man-to-man confidences, after all, require some teamwork.

"My successor, my second successor"—and Morris chuckled—"seems to be a nice guy. He's in the driving seat, all right. Just what Winifred needs."

"He appears to be very pleasant." Mr. Potter was noncommittal.

"Young for her, of course. Must be a good twenty years younger. But Winifred, like that gamy old girl in Chaucer, has a Coltes tooth. And it gives him a hold, of course. Even Winifred can't think she's thirty forever. My God, how she has aged! Looks hagridden. I wouldn't want to be in Lawrence's shoes. Anyhow, it's a big responsibility, being married to a woman with all that money."

"She hasn't," Mr. Potter reminded him, "got it yet."

"I guess her credit's still good." Morris chuckled again.

He rather fancied himself as a chuckler, Mr. Potter thought. Nevertheless, his companion's lack of co-operation was getting him down. "Guess I'll be off to bed. Maybe we can get together while you're here, for a friendly little game."

"I wouldn't," Mr. Potter surprised himself by saying.

"Huh?"

"Start a little game. It could be dangerous. There's a hole card you haven't seen yet."

"What do you mean by that?"

"The ace of spades."

And that, Mr. Potter thought, after Morris had left him, was about the corniest thing he had ever said. But he had wanted to issue a warning in terms that would be understood.

For a long time he sat before the dying fire. What hold did Morris have on Winifred? Why was Burgess sticking doggedly to the party he disliked and where he was obviously unwanted? Why had Christie been so shaken by Damon's sudden violence? What was Noah's interest in the crippled Albert Munn of San Francisco? Mr. Potter found his finger tapping out Munn's persistent rhythm (– .. – –).

There was no sense in attempting to draw conclusions on hunches, without adequate evidence. Tomorrow he would call Weston and see what he could dig up. He went quietly toward his room. The sound of low voices stopped him.

"I've given you all I can." That was Winifred, her voice shrill even when it was pitched cautiously low.

"I've got to have it." That was Morris, no longer suave.

"No!"

"Then, by God, I'll get in touch with the Recording Angel and you'll never see a penny of old Jake's money!"

Mr. Potter moved forward as noiselessly as he could. A door opened and he saw Winifred against the light, heard Lawrence say sleepily, "Where on earth have you been?" The door closed, shutting off her reply. Like an echo a second door closed, farther down the hall. Then, to Mr. Potter's considerable surprise, a third door opened and a man slipped inside. For one moment the light from his room shone on blond hair. It was Mr. John Smith, the bridegroom from San Francisco.

In his own room Mr. Potter lay awake for hours, trying to put together the puzzle. He recalled his warning to Morris: the ace of spades. It was that, all right, doubled and redoubled.

He turned restlessly, wishing that the people in the next room would stop talking and go to sleep. But when he himself fell asleep an hour later, the guarded voices were still going on in muffled tones.

6

THERE WAS mist in the morning, but the members of the guided tour, because of a tight schedule, had decided to make the excursion down the mule trail, anyhow. The Lawrence party drifted in and out of the lobby with the restlessness of vacationers who have no allotted task. After breakfast, Winifred complained of a headache and Christie went up to give her a massage, though Christie was the one who appeared to be in need of sympathetic attention. She looked as though she had not slept at all. Morris managed to get Lawrence into a game of gin rummy, a feat that aroused Mr. Potter's reluctant admiration.

Burgess was already nursing a highball. Noah had rigged up a darkroom and was developing films. Mr. and Mrs. John Smith were sharing a chair and working a crossword puzzle. Mrs. Smith was small, dark, and extremely pretty in a wide-eyed, ingenuous sort of way. Smith was in his late twenties, with blond hair, the face of a choirboy, and a general air of innocence that Mr. Potter distrusted on sight, a distrust intensified when the young man raised wide blue eyes in which there was a sardonic expression.

He was, Mr. Potter decided, an interesting young man. In fact, the bridegroom had aroused his interest from the moment when Mr. Potter had seen the raffish little MG with the soiled wedding streamer wrapped so carelessly around a wheel. A paper streamer that could survive the trip from San Francisco must be practically indestructible.

Albert Munn had been brought a breakfast tray, and Mr. Potter discovered it was in his room that the long muffled conversation had taken place the night before. Damon Knox did not appear at all. Presumably he was sulking in his tent.

Mr. Potter and Janet braved the cold mist to walk to the rim though there was little to be seen.

"It's so maddening to know it's there!" she said in exasperation.

"We'll be here until you see it," he assured her. "That's the purpose of this expedition, you know, to show Miss Christie Grand Canyon."

"I've been thinking," she said, "that Mrs. Lawrence's call for Christie might be the simple truth. All you have to do is look at her to realize that she's a wreck. Her nerves are all shot."

"To put it mildly. She's a neurotic. Being married to her must be sheer hell."

"I don't believe Mr. Lawrence feels like that," Janet said unexpectedly.

"You surely can't believe he's in love with that woman!"

"No, of course not, but I don't think he minds her—well, trying qualities."

"A euphemism, if I ever heard one."

"Just the same, he's a very relaxed sort of man. He'd

take her nerves in his stride and I believe he really makes her happy." Janet hesitated. "This sounds abominably conceited but most men at least—notice me. Mr. Lawrence hasn't a roving eye."

"He has probably learned to be discreet."

"Perhaps." She was unconvinced.

He slipped his hand under her arm. "I told you I wanted you to go away. It's still not too late."

"You think something is going to happen, don't you?"

"Something is happening." He told her of the conversation he had overheard the night before and of the bridegroom who had eavesdropped.

"Perhaps I can find out something," she suggested.

His hand tightened on her arm. "No, Janet. Absolutely no. If you are determined to provide cover for me, that will have to be the extent of your activities. If I'm going to worry about you—" He raised his head. "Look, it's beginning to clear." He stopped short.

Through slanting lines of rain the sun came out and built a radiant, multicolored arch across the canyon. They watched, motionless, until the rainbow faded.

"I'll remember this moment until the day of my death," Janet said.

"And I." He looked at her upturned face, met her with an urgency to which she responded, her hands reaching for his. Then a huge oil truck ground its way noisily up to the parking lot. "I've got to get back," he said rather breathlessly. "I want to reach Weston before he goes out to lunch. It must be nearly one in New York."

Janet looked after his rapidly retreating figure. "Damn!" she said in exasperation.

Over the long-distance telephone Weston listened to Mr. Potter's account. "My, what fun you do have! Two husbands on deck at the same time. Okay, I'll check on this Albert Munn from San Francisco. Do you think he ties in?"

"I haven't the slightest idea."

"But John Smith, San Francisco. Hell, Potter!"

"He looks like a choirboy on a bender," Mr. Potter told him helpfully. "Just married. Maybe. I'm curious about him. He drives a red MG with the California license—" He read the number from his notebook.

"Well, after all, you know about choirboys."

"This one lurks in corners. He eavesdrops. A man on his honeymoon is supposed to be single-minded."

Weston gave a loud Bronx cheer. "I've known honeymooners—" he began.

"Save it until later."

The detective laughed. "Noah Ponders is on the up and up. Good man. Always a market for his stuff. He has a commission now from *National Geographic* for a new American series. They like his work there. Nothing against him. What did you have in mind?"

"Just curiosity. I like to know about people, particularly when they keep crossing my path."

III

By the time lunch was over, the rain had gone, leaving the world fresh washed, the sky an incredibly deep blue.

Everyone, it appeared, was going on the afternoon sight-seeing bus trip.

Noah was checking his camera when Damon Knox came out of the hotel. Noah gave the younger man a wary look and his hand tightened on the camera as though to protect it.

Damon shot a half-ashamed, sidelong glance at him and then said, "Sorry I lost my temper last night. I hope I didn't hurt you."

Noah seemed incapable of resentment. "You surprised the hell out of me, but that's all. Like I said, pictures are my job."

"Better get permission next time. Fair enough?"

Noah hesitated and then shrugged. "Okay, if that's the way you want it, but most people like having their pictures taken. I can tell you that for a fact."

Damon gave him a curt nod and went on.

The bus driver was a big man with a powerful body, bronzed skin, a quiet voice, and slow, economical movements. Mr. Potter had learned to put the drivers of sight-seeing buses into two categories: the "we're all one big happy family" type; and the ones who wore themselves out with a cute line of patter. He had never been able to decide which repelled him more. But Swede Swensen was a different caliber of man. He lifted Albert Munn into the front seat and contrived to do it as unobtrusively as though he were only giving him a hand. He drove the big bus competently and, after a long slow survey of his passengers, settled down to his job without either wisecracks or any insistence that they all get on first-name terms.

Now and then he spoke quietly into the microphone before him, his words as factual, as unemotional, as he could make them, but only a fool would have failed to realize that this was a man with a lifelong love affair with the canyon. He had explored it on foot and on muleback, down the hazardous rapids of the Colorado River and by equally hazardous planes that could easily be snared in the terrific downdrafts.

"It's a right big hole in the ground," he said in his unemphatic voice. "If I were a geologist—" He broke off to suggest, "Why don't you tell them this bit, Molly?" He explained to his passengers, "Mrs. Smith is a geologist. She's been here before."

Mrs. Smith raised questioning brows to her husband.

"Why not?" he said.

She half-turned so that she could face the people in the bus: a very pretty girl who looked as though she had never had a thought in her head.

"Actually"—her clear voice was pitched to carry to the back seat—"the canyon isn't just one of the most beautiful things in the world; it's a kind of close-up of the history of what has happened to the earth since it first went whirling off into space as a separate entity; a sort of time capsule, representing hundreds of millions of years. It's all there: the signs of the oceans that flooded it, and the remains of sharks' teeth; the tokens of great rivers and molten lava; rocks that were the base of mountains; rocks that show no trace of life at all."

"Why not?" Noah asked, busily making notes.

"The heat was too great for any life to survive. Any kind of life."

"Makes you think," Lawrence said unconvincingly.

"If you go down into the canyon, and that's really the only way to have the slightest conception of its wonder and its beauty and its variety, you'll find incredible things: great red cliffs and caves and arches; the river that looks like a piece of thread from here is a roaring torrent that carries off a million tons of soil and silt a day; in fact, the Colorado River made the canyon."

"Go on," Noah prodded.

Mr. Smith grinned at his bride. "You're doing me proud, Molly."

"This used to be a land of dinosaurs," she said in her clear voice. "People, of course, are a Johnny-come-lately."

"You mean people lived here?" Noah asked.

It was Swensen's slow voice that answered. "Five Indian tribes living around here right now, some of them at the bottom of the canyon; they've been there for seven hundred years."

"Any game?" Morris asked as though to prove his sporting interest, though the idea of his hunting anything but a fourth at bridge was improbable.

"Just about anything you can name," Swensen answered.

"Do you kill much?"

"I don't like killing," drawled the big Swede. "When there are too many deer we sometimes round them up and drive them over on the Navajo Reservation. The Indians can always use fresh meat."

"I should think they could," Noah said in righteous indignation. "Downtrodden! By rights they ought to have the whole country."

"Didn't make much of it when they had it," the Swede commented.

"Well, I just don't like anyone being taken advantage of." Noah lighted a cigarette and tossed the empty package out of the window. For a moment it rested on a bush and then a puff of wind caught it and dropped it out of sight into the canyon.

"Every day," Swensen said in his even voice, "some of those young rangers you were talking to this morning risk their lives climbing around in the canyon, hauling out the trash people throw down, because it's part of their job to keep the place beautiful for tourists. And a lot of the time they have to go down to haul out the tourists, the ones who go off on their own, the smart alecks who take chances, usually with someone else's life; the ones the laws aren't made for."

Noah, rather red, made no comment.

Swensen stopped the bus. "This is a good place for taking pictures."

With the exception of Albert Munn in the front of the bus and Winifred who was in the back, everyone got off. Noah, Christie, and the Smiths were busy with their cameras. The rest were content to stare at that incredible spectacle.

No matter how often I see it, Mr. Potter thought, there's the same overwhelming shock of wonder. The sun was turning the canyon into a blaze of color: deep blues, purples, bronzes, reds, golds, greens, browns. Color that changed continually as light puffy clouds scudded through the sky. The enraptured eye traveled over rock mountains of fantastic shapes and colors. And always there was the awareness that one saw only an infinitesimal fraction of the marvel.

Janet and Mr. Potter had moved up beside Swede Swensen, who managed, while keeping a watchful eye on his flock and answering a flock of questions, to absorb the familiar beauty as though he were seeing it for the first time.

"Get off that rock," he shouted once. "It's a mile to the bottom." Burgess Holman scrambled down hastily.

Yes, Swensen said in answer to Janet's questions, he was

75

here most of the year. Twenty years or so. Getting to the point where he knew the canyon fairly well. There was a lot of canyon. You got to know it better, of course, when you had time to live with it. But tourists tried to get in a couple of quick looks. Some of them spent more time buying postcard views to prove they'd been there than looking at the canyon itself. That young lady, Mrs. Smith she was now, had come here for several summers. She was a trained geologist. To see her you wouldn't think she was a scientist, would you?

"Do you know her well?" Mr. Potter asked casually.

"I see a good bit of her whenever she comes to the canyon. Molly Coleman she was before she married. She knows a lot I don't and I know some she doesn't, so we hit it off."

Janet glanced at Mr. Potter as they started back to the bus. "Do I display signs of jealousy?"

"No. But you might develop a friendship with Mrs. Smith. Only don't get trapped into making any girlish confidences. She looks as though she couldn't understand a television spectacular but she's smart as a whip."

"And married to Saintly Sam," Janet said. "She could have done better than that."

"All is not gold that goes over the dam," he warned her.

"And a stitch in time gathers no moss. All right, I'll watch it."

Slowly the sightseers drifted back. Morris was one of the first to return to the bus and Mr. Potter was struck again by the anomaly of this man's presence on a sightseeing bus. For a moment the gambler stood trying to catch his ex-wife's eyes but she was looking at the handbag on her lap, smoothing it, turning it nervously over and over.

Lawrence got in with Burgess, holding his arm with a

solicitude that surprised Mr. Potter until he noticed that Burgess was staggering. The older man eased him into a seat and then went back to join his wife. They held a whispered conversation, looking uneasily at the boy who appeared to be carrying a great deal more than he could handle.

The last to return to the bus were Noah, Christie, and Damon Knox. Noah and the nurse apparently had struck up an acquaintance based on their mutual interest in photography, and they sat together, eagerly discussing technicalities. Damon took a long look at his cousin, made a grimace of distaste, and dropped into the front seat beside Albert Munn.

Swensen closed the door and pressed the starter. It was several minutes before the passengers were aware that something was wrong. Swensen spoke into the mike beside the driver's seat.

"I'm sorry, folks. We seem to have developed an oil leak. I'll send out a call for cars to take you back to the hotel. If you want a refund—"

"We want to see the canyon," Winifred said tartly. "That's what we're here for."

"We can make the same trip tomorrow, darling," Lawrence said placatingly.

"Well, now," Swensen was embarrassed, "we've got tomorrow afternoon's trip booked up. Maybe the next day."

"We don't even know how long we are staying. James darling, you ought to talk to the manager. Such poor management. How they expect to get tourists—"

"There's a full moon tonight," Christie said quickly. "Why can't we come then? Would you mind, Mr. Swensen?"

There was a pause and then the driver said reluctantly,

"Guess I owe you that much. Yes, I'll make the trip. The thing is, moonlight doesn't really reach very far. You aren't going to see much canyon."

Moonlight, Winifred exclaimed, would be wonderful.

Perhaps it was her capitulation, her willingness to abandon making an issue of the situation, that impelled everyone to agree to make the night trip.

When the same group climbed, four hours later, onto the bus, Mr. Potter was somewhat surprised to see that Albert Munn still made one of the party.

As Swensen had warned them, the moonlight, beautiful as it was in itself, did not touch the canyon. "It's like I told you," he said once, apologetically; "you can't see much and you can't get any pictures."

"Any objection to our trying?" Noah asked. "I've got some fine effects by moonlight."

"That's up to you," Swensen said. "Only remember that you've got to watch your step out there."

Noah was already waiting for the door to open, with Christie behind him, taking her camera out of its case. Morris, still hellbent on appearing an insatiable sightseer, started to leave the bus. Then Lawrence stood up.

"James," Winifred protested shrilly, "do you think you'd better? Heights make you so dizzy and there's no railing."

"Don't worry, my sweet."

"I wish you wouldn't."

He blew her a kiss and his wife simpered. That's odd, Mr. Potter thought, it's the first time I've ever really seen anyone simper. I thought it was a defunct Victorianism like the wringing of hands and attacks of the vapors.

Damon stood up and Burgess lurched forward to join him. Swensen asked a low-voice question and Damon an-

78

swered. Young Mr. and Mrs. Smith were already climbing down.

"Do you want to get out here?" Mr. Potter asked.

Janet shook her head. "What's the point? I can't see anything." She leaned forward to speak to the driver. "This has been very kind of you."

At a shout from Noah he switched off the lights in the bus. "It was my fault. I should have checked the oil gauge on the bus this afternoon. Owed it to you folks. I don't mind the extra trip. What worries me is that kid with the load on. I shouldn't have let him get out but he was all set to make a row and the other young fellow said he'd keep an eye on him."

"Can they really take pictures by moonlight?" Mr. Potter asked.

"Ponders can. I know his stuff. He's one of the best. About the others, I wouldn't know. Moonlight is tricky. If you're not used to it, you can be fooled by shadows. Many a time I've taken a bush for a bear and once"—he chuckled —"I took a bear for a bush. Now that was really something."

"What happened?" Janet demanded.

He laughed. "Nothing exciting, like you tourists always want. We just sheered off each other and grunted and took to our heels."

There was a high scream from outside, followed by a startled cry and confused shouting: "I was pushed . . . I nearly went over . . . ! O God, someone has gone over!"

As Swensen switched on the bus lights and got out, Janet clutched Mr. Potter's arm. "Burgess! Do you think he fell? He's never been so drunk before that he didn't know what he was doing."

And then Winifred's voice rose from the back of the bus.

"Christie! It's Christie!" The words broke off in a bubbling gasp as the nurse got on the bus.

Christie was white but she was composed and her voice was steadying. "I'm here. I'm all right."

At Swensen's orders, unstressed but not to be disobeyed, the others were all climbing back on the bus.

"A terrible thing," Lawrence babbled as he hastened back to his wife.

Morris moved forward blindly, seeming to grope his way to a vacant seat.

Damon steadied Burgess who looked as though he had been shocked back into sobriety. Young Smith kept his arm around his wife who was sobbing.

"I tell you, Jack, someone pushed against me."

"It's all right, darling. It's all right now."

But it wasn't all right. After a wait that seemed interminable, Swensen got in and closed the door. Noah Ponders was missing.

7

"You're sure," Lawrence called from the back of the bus, "that there's no chance of saving him? He might be hanging onto a bush or something."

"I had a good look around with that flashlight," Swensen said in a tone of finality. "It's a mile to the bottom where he went down."

After that no one spoke until they had returned to the hotel. The resourceful manager, appalled as he was by the disaster, said that there would be sandwiches and drinks provided by the hotel, in the dining room in thirty minutes. He urged them all to come. They would need something to build them up after their shock.

Swensen exchanged looks with the manager. "Best thing you could do, folks," he told them.

It was then that Winifred went into a fit of screaming hysterics, appalling to watch, and Christie, with Lawrence's help, got her up to her room. Burgess pulled a flask out of his pocket and took a long drink. Damon, watching him, was about to protest, then shrugged his shoulders.

Burgess was still sober enough to be aware of his cousin's disapproval. "You certainly had it in for that guy. At least he can't take any more pictures of you now."

The color drained from Damon's face. "Just what do you mean by that?"

"There's been enough trouble for one day," Morris intervened sharply. "For God's sake, can't you two apes grow up?"

"Mother's Second as referee. That's a nice touch. A very nice touch."

"I was speaking for your own good, Damon. Last night you tried to knock the man down without provocation and a lot of people saw it. The quieter both of you young fools keep from now on the better it will be for everybody."

"What's wrong, Teddy?" Burgess's voice was thick. "Afraid we're going to spoil your little game?"

Morris's eyes slid from the Smiths to Mr. Potter to Janet and back to his tormenter. "You're stewed to the gills, Burgess. Why don't you go to your room and try to sober up?"

With unexpected docility Burgess got to his feet and then toppled over. Between them, Morris and Damon hauled him away. With the exception of the bride and groom, who were whispering together, and Albert Munn, who sat hunched over the great fire, there was no one left in the lobby but Swensen, who leaned against the desk, his face grim.

"May I join the rescue party?" Mr. Potter asked him.

Swensen shook his head. "This is our job. It's easier without amateurs getting in the way." There was no criticism in his tone, just plain statement of fact. The door opened and four young park rangers came in, equipped with ropes and tackle. "Let's go."

"How did it happen?" one of the rangers asked.

"Someone shoved against him."

"Deliberately, you mean?" The ranger was startled.

"I don't know. Can't see any reason for it. Perhaps someone got dizzy or just lost his balance. Miss Coleman— Mrs. Smith—said she felt someone jolt against her." Swensen looked toward the bride and groom.

"We were all in a group near the bus," the girl said, her voice shaking. "Mr. Ponders wanted the bus lights shut off so he could get a moonlight picture and we couldn't see much. People jostled a bit because they didn't want to move out too close to the rim. Then something knocked against me. I'd have pitched over if Jack hadn't caught me. And then I heard that terrible yell. It was—" She closed her eyes and groped for her husband's hand.

"Maybe Ponders stumbled," he said, "and brushed against you."

"Ponders knew his way around," Swensen put in. "I've seen his stuff in the *Geographic* for years. He shot pictures under water and from airplanes, he followed mountain climbers and steeplejacks. He knew all the tricks and he wasn't careless." Mr. Potter noticed Swensen's use of the past tense.

"Someone got rattled. Is that what you think?" Smith asked.

"Rattled? Well, maybe. That guy Holman was so drunk he was staggering." There was anger in Swensen's quiet voice. "His cousin swore that he'd keep an eye on him. I suppose they'll call it accident." The door closed behind the rescue team.

"Want to lie down, Molly?" Smith asked.

"No, I'm too jittery."

Mr. Potter turned to Smith. "Have you any idea in what order people were standing out there?"

"You are Hiram Potter, aren't you?" Shrewd eyes looked out from the round, choirboy face. "No, I haven't any idea how we were standing. Sort of grouped together, I think. I didn't notice anyone but Molly, who was on my left. I have an idea that Ponders was on her other side, with Miss Christie beside him. I had the impression of a sort of stumbling run and then Ponders screamed like a woman. I thought at first it was the nurse who had gone. From the back they looked alike, you know; same size, slacks, short coat, dark cropped hair." Smith's eyes caught and held Mr. Potter's. "Quite a bit alike." When he observed that Mr. Potter had no comment to make he reached for his wife's hand and pulled her to her feet.

"Come and fix your face and then we'll take the manager up on the drinks and sandwiches."

"I couldn't."

"Yes, you can. Come on, baby."

At last Janet turned to Mr. Potter. She was white and shaken. "You don't think it was an accident, do you?"

He shook his head.

"But why kill a harmless man like Noah Ponders?"

"We don't know whether he was killed as Noah Ponders or as Bertha Christie. Smith is right; they did look alike from the back. I mistook Miss Christie for Ponders and Mrs. Lawrence mistook him for the nurse."

"But suppose it wasn't a mistake," she insisted. "Why would anyone kill a harmless photographer?"

"There's just one possibility that I can see: the fantastic attack Damon Knox made on him. Apparently Ponders got an indiscreet picture of our handsome boy at some time or other."

The unnecessary disparagement of Damon's good looks made Janet flick him a quick look. She was cheered but she did not pursue her advantage.

"You know, Hiram, I can't believe Noah Ponders was the kind of man who would capitalize on a thing like that."

"Nor I," he admitted. "If there is anything wrong we'll find out, sooner or later."

"Later," she said somberly.

"I know. If Ponders was killed by mistake, Miss Christie is still in danger. In great danger."

"Can't you do anything, Hiram?"

"I'll talk to her. I'll try to make her tell me what she knows or suspects. After that, there would be no advantage in anyone attempting to silence her. Personally, I think it is Damon she is protecting. But if she suspects that he tried to kill her tonight, she's bound to have a drastic change of heart."

"You think she really knows something about all this?"

He made a helpless gesture. There were, he pointed out, some peculiar factors. If anyone was thoroughly conversant with the Maybrick peculiarities, it would be Christie who had devoted much of her professional life to them. They all, with the notable exception of Burgess, kept harping on her loyalty. And, he added reluctantly, she had a big settlement coming to her out of the Stendel estate.

"But, Hiram," Janet protested, "she wouldn't—"

He didn't, he assured her, think so either. What worried him most was not the possibility of Christie's complicity in a series of crimes, it was that someone must know she had removed a glass containing traces of white arsenic from Stendel's room after his death.

Janet studied him with concern. "You look awful," she

said candidly.

"Noah Ponders was an inveterate bore but I doubt if he ever harmed anyone in his life, and he loved living. At this moment I'm as close to being in a killing rage as I've ever been in my life. I'm not good company."

"Then you aren't going to accept the manager's invitation for sandwiches and drinks."

"Oh, yes, I am. I want to know who comes down and how they act."

"Then I'll clean up and join you later."

When he went upstairs, Christie was coming out of the Lawrences' room. She put her finger to her lips and closed the door softly. "She's asleep at last; I've never known her to be in such a state. If she isn't considerably improved by tomorrow, I'm going to insist on a doctor. I can't take the responsibility."

"Very wise of you. May I speak to you for a moment, Miss Christie?"

She looked surprised but agreed. He opened his door and waited for her to precede him. When she was seated, he offered her a cigarette, which she refused.

He spoke quietly. "Miss Christie, I came out here at the request of Dr. Holman."

Her big competent hands clenched convulsively and then relaxed. "Why?"

"I think you know why. Because he believes you may be in danger."

"I!" She was obviously dumbfounded. "That's preposterous."

"Is it? I wonder whether it has occurred to you that Noah Ponders may have been pushed off the rim tonight in mistake for you."

The blunt words filled her face with shock and terror.

"Oh, no," she whispered. "Oh, no!"

"I'm very much afraid it is 'Oh, yes.' Miss Christie, there is a possibility, a probability, as you very well know, that Jake Stendel was murdered. There's more than a likelihood that his physician, Dr. Mourner, was killed before he could have any second thoughts about that death certificate."

There was complete incredulity in her face. "But Dr. Mourner's death was an accident!"

"Was it? Brakes failed on a car whose brakes had just been checked. All evidence of tampering disappeared when the car was destroyed by fire within twelve hours. Two other people died and two children were permanently disabled in that accident. And tonight we have had the fifth fatality in a long and ugly chain."

"I don't believe it," she said through stiff lips. "Noah Ponders simply lost his balance. There was very little room at the rim."

"He was a nice guy, Miss Christie; well-meaning, kindly, and he loved life. If you had told all that you know or guess about Stendel's death, Ponders might be enjoying life at this moment instead of—being where he is."

"That's brutal," she said angrily.

"I am aware of that. But I must impress on you that you have got to talk about what happened in San Francisco when Stendel died. It may be your only chance."

The nurse had learned years before to guard her expression, not to betray her thoughts to the searching, anguished eyes of patients. She sat for a long time looking at her scrubbed, short-nailed hands. What was going on behind that quiet face: fear of discovery? fear for her future safety? incredulity? a coming to terms with a totally new and shocking idea?

87

It was a long time before she looked squarely at him. "I don't really know what happened, Mr. Potter."

"You found a glass that contained white arsenic. That glass you removed and later destroyed. Someone must be wondering what you really did with it. Who was in the house at the time?"

"Mrs. Lawrence, her son Damon, her nephew Burgess, the servants."

"Wasn't Lawrence there?"

"No, he'd gone down to Santa Barbara to inspect some property. A new housing development, I think." Color began to seep back into her face. "Don't you see, it couldn't be either of the Lawrences. He was away when Mr. Stendel died and tonight, as you know yourself, she didn't leave the bus when Mr. Ponders fell. Anyhow, she couldn't have damaged Dr. Mourner's car. Not possibly. She hasn't driven for years; I doubt if she ever knew anything about brakes except that they are supposed to stop a car."

She found his silence unbearable. At length she sighed in capitulation. "Mr. Morris was there that day. He wanted to see Mrs. Lawrence."

"Had he ever been there before?"

"Several times," she said reluctantly. "When Mr. Lawrence was out of town."

II

Sandwiches and drinks had been lavishly supplied and served buffet-style on the big center table, but for some reason the guests, after serving themselves, took separate tables, scattered like islands in the South Pacific, each wearing his rue with a difference.

The greatest difference, of course, was the table where

88

Morris sat alone, the table at which, the night before, Noah Ponders had faced him, talking with his usual exuberance, his unconquerable zest in the love of living. Morris was profoundly shaken. Though he drank deeply he barely touched the sandwiches with which he had heaped his plate. Once he turned to look at Mr. Potter, a queer expression on his face.

Albert Munn, too, sat alone, with a book propped open before him as a kind of barricade against any possible conversational overtures. The Smiths talked together in low tones, their honeymoon radiance subdued not only by the tragedy but by the silence that hung over the dining room like an uneasy cloud. Mr. Potter had selected a table where he and Janet could sit side by side, both looking out over the room.

Christie came in, followed by Lawrence and the two young men. Burgess had pulled himself together in a remarkably short time.

"I guess we could all do with a drink," Lawrence said, looking at the buffet spread out on the center table. He looked doubtfully at Burgess. "Well, maybe not."

Burgess poured bourbon into a highball glass, added water, very little water.

"Why don't you skip it tonight, boy?" Lawrence suggested casually.

"Why should I?" Burgess asked with the drunk's easy belligerence.

"After all, you were pretty well out on your feet an hour or so ago. Doesn't do to give people anything to talk about."

The heavy brows rose. Burgess looked at Lawrence for a moment. "Oh, no, you don't," he said softly. "Don't get any ideas."

"I don't mean that you're drunk now," Lawrence told him with patent insincerity.

"You just think I was in such bad shape tonight I knocked that guy over the rim. Uh-huh."

"I didn't say that," Lawrence protested.

"Well, don't. There's only one person here who has had practice at knocking Ponders around and that is Damon, the poor man's Hamlet."

Damon gave his cousin a lazy smile. "Let him talk," he advised his stepfather. "Let him set it to music if he can."

Christie said nothing at all. She ate her way stolidly through some sandwiches and then excused herself. She would just look in on Mrs. Lawrence before she went to bed. "Try not to wake her when you go up; she's overwrought and she needs her rest."

"No wonder," Damon said gently. He turned all his charm on the nurse. "She thought it was you, of course. When you got on the bus, safe and sound, it must have been quite a shock."

On the whole, it was as unpleasant a situation as Mr. Potter could remember, but at least it was mercifully brief. They were all in a hurry to finish and get away from each other.

By ten o'clock the lobby was empty except for Mr. Potter. The fire had died down and the room was growing chilly. For a long time he sat staring at the embers. Once again a man had been killed and once again it would be called accident. But had Noah Ponders died as himself or as Bertha Christie? Winifred had assumed that it was Christie from the moment that terrible scream had been heard, a point that Damon had been quick to grasp. Lawrence had had to help Burgess onto the bus during the afternoon trip because he lacked co-ordination; he had appeared to be practically out on his feet when he returned to the hotel after the night's excursion. Just how drunk had he actually been?

Morris had been in a state of shock when he got back on the bus. Morris who had been at Stendel's house on the day of his death; who had, apparently, been there several times in Lawrence's absence. From San Francisco to Las Vegas to Grand Canyon. He seemed to stay at Winifred's heels with deadly persistence.

The guileless Mrs. Smith was positive that someone had shoved against her. Or so she had said. Mr. Potter found himself wondering about the Smiths as he had from the moment when he had seen that frankly unbelievable paper streamer around a wheel, since he had seen the cupid's bow of lipstick on Smith's cheek when the couple had returned from the rim with Christie and Lawrence the night before. Mrs. Smith wore very little make-up. They were overplaying their parts.

Mr. Potter went upstairs for his overcoat. Tonight there were neither voices nor lights. He left the hotel and walked out to the rim. For a long time he stood staring at the canyon by moonlight. What a pity Janet wasn't here to share this with him.

You couldn't look into the magnificence of space and time and lie to youself. There was no place for evasion here. He was in love with Janet Grant. And what he was going to do about it he couldn't imagine. He was thirty-six and he had, though somewhat belatedly, built a life that satisfied him. Probably an egocentric life. He was ready to concede the point. People interested him profoundly but he didn't want them too close to him, he didn't want them all the time. He didn't want any woman on a permanent basis, a woman who would always be there. Always was a long time. On the other hand, there was no satisfaction in contemplating a life in which there would never again be Janet. Never was a bleak sort of word. He stood alone with the canyon and the moon and himself. This wonder was enough, wasn't it? Or was it?

A cloud moved across the face of the moon, leaving him in darkness. For a few minutes he stood waiting for the light to return, too wakeful to go back to his room and to bed. At length he reached for a cigarette, struck a match. The wind blew it out.

"Damn!" he said aloud, heard a startled gasp behind him, and started to turn.

8

THE BLOW caught him between the shoulders and he
pitched forward, arms flailing. They'll call it accident, he
thought bitterly, and his fingers touched a bush, clung to
it, his face plunged into it; his feet, scrabbling frantically,
grated on rock. One tentative hand dangled in space, the
other clutched the bush harder. He had probably loosened
it.

Even if he dared move his head he could have seen nothing. He might be within feet of a path; he might be hanging over space. Inch by inch, he clawed himself closer to
the face of the cliff, away from the abyss. He was on a ledge
that could not be more than eighteen inches wide. His face
was in the bush and he dared not move for fear he'd lose
an eye or dislodge some rocks or tear the bush out by the
roots.

A light shone down, blinding him. "God! Don't move,
man. Hang on."

And that, Mr. Potter thought, pressing himself against

the cliff wall, was about the most unnecessary order anyone had ever issued. There were pounding feet; shouts; a circle of lights; then something scraped on rock, hands were fastening a rope around him.

"You're all right, but take it easy. No sudden moves." That was the calm voice of Swede Swensen.

"Keep my arms free. I can help myself." Mr. Potter cautiously lifted his face out of the bush. "I don't think I broke anything. Just knocked out my wind."

The big Swede stood beside him, guiding as the rope pulled him slowly upward into the waiting hands of two park rangers. Someone held his arms, his feet were planted on solid ground. He took a long, uneven breath.

The Swede followed easily. "If you had to jump over, you should have picked a spot that didn't have a ledge eight feet below the rim."

"How did you find me?"

The Swede ducked his head and Mr. Potter turned to look into John Smith's seraphic face.

"Just happened to see you fall." The hell you did, thought Mr. Potter. "I let out a yell for Swensen who was going into the hotel with a couple of rangers."

"Any luck?" Mr. Potter asked quickly.

Swensen shook his head. "Not a sign so far. The team is still working on it, of course, but there are no ledges where Ponders went down." He turned and walked heavily away, followed by the rangers.

Smith strolled beside Mr. Potter toward the hotel, but, though he looked at him several times, he did not attempt to talk, to ask questions. The manager was alone in the lobby. He saw Mr. Potter's scraped cheek, his torn coat, and he was shaken out of his usual soothing imperturbability.

94

"What in God's name happened to you?"

"Only God knows."

After a long, hot shower he felt better. He was warm at last and the fear that had gripped him during those moments on the ledge was gone. He did not attempt to deny that he had been afraid, though even at the time his strongest emotion had been impotent fury at the thought that someone had got away with murder again.

An inventory of the damages showed that his face, as he had expected, looked as though a cat had clawed it. One shin was bleeding from a shallow cut, his knees were scraped and discolored and swollen. The nails of one hand had been broken. On the whole, not so bad. Not bad at all.

He pulled on a warm dressing gown, locked his door and, feeling a trifle melodramatic, took a small automatic from his suitcase. This was the first time he had ever planned to go armed on a case, but it was also the first time anyone had ever tried to push him into Grand Canyon.

He poured a drink of Haig & Haig, lighted a cigarette, and switched off the reading lamp, looking out on the dark night. Someone had followed him, had not dared move in the moonlight, and had taken instant advantage of the sudden darkness. He had helped by lighting the match to pinpoint his position. How much had Smith seen? And who the hell was the enigmatic John Smith?

Mr. Potter made a fresh drink, lighted another cigarette, and went over the case from the time when Dr. Holman had first told him the story. Everything had stemmed from the death of Jake Stendel, and there could be little doubt not only that it was murder but that the killer was now in the hotel. The most damning factor was that Winifred had assumed at once that it was Christie who had fallen to her death, and she had collapsed completely when she learned that the nurse was alive and uninjured.

But Winifred had not left the bus when Ponders was killed. She could have had no direct hand in his death. Was she working then in collusion with someone else? The obvious one was Lawrence, but Lawrence had been absent from San Francisco when Stendel and Dr. Mourner had been killed. Damon? Possible, of course, but Damon loathed his mother and he was the last person likely to aid and abet anything she did.

Burgess? Possible, again, but unlikely. Janet had been accurate in her summing up of the young man. Behind the face of a rather brutal thug there was no strength, nothing but a kind of spiteful resentment against life and a corroding jealousy of his handsome cousin. Still there had been the "accidents" during his truncated college career; there was his tenacious insistence on remaining with the Lawrence party.

Morris? But what reason could he have unless he feared that Christie would reveal his presence in San Francisco at the time of Stendel's murder?

Mr. Potter yawned, drained his glass, and went to bed. He must have scared hell out of someone to risk that attempt to kill him. It would be comforting to have some inkling as to which one it was. He hoped that he had put the fear of God into Christie. Whether or not she was willing to believe that she could be a victim, from now on she would be observant, on her guard. He moved uneasily. Damn it all, the thing felt wrong. Looking back he wasn't sure whether the nurse had presented Morris to him as a suspect or as a red herring.

Shaving next morning proved to be an uncomfortable business, which opened some of the cuts and started them bleeding. Surveying his face in the mirror, Mr. Potter decided that he looked as though he had scraped his way through a barbed-wire fence. A fresh bandage took care of the cut on his shin but his knees were still swollen and walking was painful. It could, he reminded himself, have been a lot worse. He might have a couple of broken legs right now and still be grateful.

When he went down to the lobby, he found Janet and Molly Smith talking as volubly as though they were old friends. In some alarm he wondered what information the guileless bride had managed to extract from Janet who would be no match for her.

"And where," Janet demanded, "did you meet that buzz saw?"

"Just a prickly bush," he assured her lightly. "Fell over it in the dark. Awkward fellow."

"I suppose the bush has a black eye. I hope."

He grinned at her and shook his head at Molly. "Suspicious natures you women have. I see I'll have to improve my technique."

"You'll have to improve your story." Janet saw his expression and changed what she was about to say. "I'll have coffee with you while you eat breakfast. Everyone else finished long ago."

"Where are they?" he asked sharply and was aware that Molly was giving him a speculative look.

"Just strolling around. No one wanted to take the morning bus trip." As he forestalled the waiter and pulled out a chair for her in the dining room she said, "You're limping."

"Nothing serious. I just—lost my balance and took a fall."

"Well, if you won't tell me, I suppose you won't."

"Any news of Ponders?"

"The rangers hunted all night and, so far as I know, they are still down there."

"Any comments?"

She shook her head. "No one has even mentioned him. It might never have happened. But no one wanted to take the morning sightseeing bus trip; they shied like a nervous horse at the idea. They're planning to go on to Las Vegas tomorrow."

"Who are?"

"The Lawrence party. Oh, and Mr. Morris said as long as the group was breaking up, he'd go, too."

"The whole works then." Mr. Potter got up rather stiffly. "I'd like to run down to Flagstaff and make a private telephone call. Would you care to come along?"

"Of course."

As he started to open the car door, she asked, "Would you like me to drive?"

"You don't mind?"

"No, I'd enjoy it."

He got in and stretched his legs in relief as he fastened his seat belt. Janet drove competently, refusing to raise her eyes from the road even when the tantalizing views of the canyon came in sight. After a while he looked at her profile and decided that he had better not. The less conscious of her beauty he was, the better off he would be. She didn't chatter or make demands on his attention, a rare quality in a woman.

"You're a restful person, Janet."

"That's what you think," she said darkly. "I will not ask questions. I will not ask questions. I will not ask questions. But I am dying by inches."

He laughed outright, then sobered. "Janet, you'll have to go home. Things are getting out of control."

"I realized that when I saw the sag in your right-hand jacket pocket. You're carrying a gun of some sort."

"Well, gents' clothing doesn't come equipped with shoulder holsters as a rule," he complained. "But if it's that conspicuous I'll fix something better before we go back to the hotel."

"Maybe you'd be wiser to leave it as it is, a kind of fair warning."

He was suspicious. "What were you and the bride discussing with so much animation?"

Janet tried to speak coolly but her voice shook. "She told me that someone deliberately tried to kill you last night."

"And what was her opinion of that little performance?"

"Don't, for God's sake, try to be flippant about it! It was your life, Hiram, and you nearly lost it."

"Sorry. I just didn't want you to worry."

"Worry!" Janet said in a tone of fury. "Any woman could tell you that the worst thing is not knowing."

"Come on," he cajoled her, "you're full of information and bursting to tell me. Don't hold out."

"Molly said her husband had gone for a walk." Janet answered his thoughts as though he had spoken them aloud. "I know. I didn't believe her, either. He saw you standing out at the rim and heard someone behind him. Just as he turned around, the moon went under a cloud and he couldn't see a thing. Then a match flared and he heard a shout. That was you. Someone raced past him, nearly knocking him down.

"He didn't have a chance to discover who it was, because, naturally, his first idea was to see whether you could be saved. Of course, by the time he had found you and hailed Swensen and the rangers, whoever attacked you had gone. The manager had been out of the lobby for a few moments and saw no one come in. Jack Smith went upstairs and listened at doors but he didn't hear anyone moving."

"Anything more?"

"Molly asked a lot about you: whether you had any enemies, how well you knew Noah Ponders. Things like that."

"A very curious young woman."

"When someone tries to murder a man, almost anyone would wonder why," Janet said rather tartly. "And it wasn't a cross-examination; she knew I'd be worried. We're supposed to be engaged, if you remember."

Mr. Potter smoothly bypassed the challenge in her voice, a feat in which he was beginning to acquire some practice. It was bad enough for her to be so lovely to look at, but her staunch, unswerving partisanship made his position more and more untenable. He wanted her as he had never wanted anything in his life.

"Anything else?" he said with admirable detachment.

"She assumed we were all old friends, the Lawrences and the two boys and you and I, and that we had met here by arrangement. I told her you had never known any of them before and that we had come out on the spur of the moment to get away from the press."

"Do you think she believed you?"

"I don't know," Janet admitted. "Oh, there was one

funny thing. She asked if we had noticed the queer way Mr. Munn and Mr. Morris watch each other. She said it made her think of amateur theatricals and people waiting for cues. And she said there didn't seem to be any love lost between Morris and Damon, and that Morris had been furious when Damon struck poor Ponders."

"For a young couple absorbed in each other, the Smiths do a powerful lot of noticing, as my old nurse used to say."

"At that point," Janet said, "I went all girlish about our love affair and kept the conversation strictly on your charms, because I didn't know what you would want me to say. She reciprocated by raving about Saintly Sam."

"Did you find out anything about him?"

"He's not a scientist, though I don't know what his job is, and they really are just married. That's all I got out of her." Janet laughed ruefully. "I'm not much good at this sort of thing. Molly seems to babble along like a Fourth of July oration but she—well, you know how an octopus protects itself by throwing out that inky stuff."

"I shouldn't have suggested those girlish confidences. Sorry about that, Janet."

"Next time I'll do better, but it would help if I had any idea of what you want to know."

"You steer clear of the Smiths."

She raised an eyebrow. "Do I detect a faint touch of proprietorship?"

"I'm trying to keep you out of trouble."

"It's good training. Perhaps I shouldn't discourage it."

For all his determination to ignore her mockery he found himself grinning. In Flagstaff, he left her in a restaurant while he called Weston. When he had finished talking the detective let out a low whistle.

"Noah Ponders killed and an attempt made on you!

What the hell goes on? You had better put the police on this; it's out of hand."

"There's no way of identifying the one who pushed me. Not a scrap of evidence."

"Just the same," Weston said, "I'm going to see O'Toole, give him a rundown of the whole story, and let him come up with some suggestions. Aside from the fact that you are now a marked man, you can't guard the nurse by yourself, particularly in a place like Las Vegas where everyone is on the move."

"Anything new at your end?"

"Roland Adams, Stendel's executor, is a tartar. I called him in San Francisco and he listened to what I had to tell him and then shut up like a clam. I tried to say there was dirty work at the crossroads and he froze me out. Dr. Holman had already been in touch with him about the alleged murder of his client and the alleged tampering with Dr. Mourner's car. He had been informed of the presence of Mrs. Lawrence's second husband in San Francisco at the time of his client's death. Up to now he had been regarded as entirely competent to handle his own affairs and those entrusted to him by the late Mr. Stendel, without outside advise. And thank me very much."

"Well," Mr. Potter said thoughtfully.

"I tell you, Potter, the guy is inhuman. He never turned a hair."

"That's what Dr. Holman told me. Anything else?"

"You may pin a medal on my breast at any time, though I shy at being kissed on both cheeks. Believe it or not, I found your John Smith. Voter in San Francisco. Has an MG with the right license number. Married Mary Coleman, also of San Francisco, ten days ago."

"Good work!"

"Good?" Weston protested indignantly. "Magnificent!"

"Did you find out anything more about the third husband, Damon Knox?"

"The marriage broke up over in Paris years ago. Winifred got the divorce and came back alone. He returned to America some time last autumn."

"Hell!" Mr. Potter's dismay was heartfelt. "So he's around, too. That means he could still be in the picture. Try to find out where he is now, will you?"

"Do you know what this is costing you? For a search like that I might have to cover the country."

"It's cheaper than the one-way ticket to hell that someone seems to have bought me." Mr. Potter tapped his finger idly against the glass wall of the telephone booth and realized that he was tapping out Munn's compulsive rhythm. "I'll call you from Las Vegas."

"You're going ahead with this, then?"

"Of course," Mr. Potter said in surprise.

"Take care of yourself."

"That's what I do best," Mr. Potter assured him, laughing, but he didn't do as well with Janet. She listened to all his arguments and then said, "I'm going with you to Las Vegas."

"Can you provide a plausible story to account for our going at this time, along with the general exodus?"

She countered, "Can you?" When he was silent, she thought for a moment, winged brows drawn together. How often, the man across from her wondered, does anyone see beauty like this? Sunlight blazed down on the pale-gold hair, touched the flawless skin, the long dark eyes, the mouth that could be so warm, so responsive.

"Where's that telephone?" she asked suddenly. "I'm going to call Cass."

9

THAT NIGHT there was still no word from the rangers. The members of the mule-trail party came in, tired but exultant, and went to their rooms; once more the hotel was filled with bustle and excitement, talk and laughter. By tacit agreement, they were not told about the death of Noah Ponders; his presumed death, the manager suggested anxiously.

Christie had done Winifred's packing as well as her own and the whole party had gathered around the fire. Lawrence ordered drinks and endeavored to impart a kind of cheerfulness to the group, a cheerfulness in which, to Mr. Potter's surprise, he was given aid and comfort by Burgess Holman. Even Winifred had regained her usual querulous manner, yesterday's storm forgotten.

The manager came in search of Janet. There was a long-distance call for her. When she returned she was frowning.

"Really," she told Mr. Potter in exasperation, her voice raised so that it carried clearly, "Cass is impossible. What do you think that brother of mine has done now? After promising to join us here, he says he's caught cold and he needs sunshine; anyhow, he's seen the canyon before."

"Then he's not coming?"

"He's leaving for Las Vegas. Said he needed hot, dry air and a little excitement, and he'd meet us there. Sometimes I'd like to throttle him." ˑ

Sometimes, Mr. Potter thought, I'd like to throttle you. He looked up to see Smith watching Janet with an expression of cold, sharp intelligence.

"Marvelous!" Winifred exclaimed. "These things are always more fun when there's a party. Let's have a picnic lunch put up and we can all stop somewhere on the road. You'll love Las Vegas, Christie. The Strip is simply fabulous."

Uninvited, Morris brought his drink over and joined the party. "Ever done any gambling, Mr. Munn?" he asked the quiet man in the corner.

"I tried my luck once at Monte Carlo."

"Enjoy it?"

"Not particularly. I'm not a lucky man. My chief interest lay in watching the gamblers. That's where the real drama comes in. Always hopeful but in the long run—" He was shaken by a sudden fit of coughing. "In the long run the house wins. Law of averages or something, like insurance."

"It depends on how you play it," Morris told him.

"Your cough is worse than it was this morning," Damon said to Munn. "Why didn't you get out in the sun today?"

"I feel the cold. I've lived too long in a warm climate."

"Why not try Las Vegas? The hot desert air ought to do the trick, as Miss Grant's brother says."

"That's an idea, but I don't drive. It's a long time since

I've driven." Munn's hand tightened on the stick. "Last time I went motoring—this happened to me."

"You are wise not to try it," Morris put in. "The drive across the desert is beastly uncomfortable. Baking heat. A great strain."

Unexpectedly Damon turned to Mr. Potter. "I should think that hot sunny air was indicated, wouldn't you? Our car is filled but—look here, Mr. Potter, don't you have room for an extra passenger?"

For sheer unadulterated impertinence, Mr. Potter thought, you take the cake. Using me to settle your score with Morris. To his surprise, Munn did not reject the suggestion. Instead, he turned to Mr. Potter with a questioning expression.

Aware that he was being maneuvered, there was still nothing to be done without deliberate rudeness. "We'd be delighted." Mr. Potter saw a curious exchange of glances between Morris and Munn. The latter seemed to be saying, "My trick, I believe."

II

When Mr. Potter went downstairs early the following morning, Swede Swensen was alone in the lobby. There was still no trace of Noah Ponders.

"He was a good guy," the Swede said. "He talked too much, of course; most people do. But he liked life and he made other people like it. There was no harm in him." Behind the slow voice there was deadly anger.

The two men stood in silence while Mr. Potter waited. At length Swensen said, "That fall you had last night." He paused again. "Might be wise to keep an eye on your friends."

"I intend to. I take it you didn't see who it was."

"Whoever it was must have ducked out of sight until we got busy at the rim. All we knew was that someone had gone over. Another—accident. By the time Smith told us there had been someone around it was too late." He ruminated for a moment. "Only guests here were Mr. Lawrence's party, that guy Morris, the Smiths, poor Munn, your fiancée. I know Molly and any man she'd marry would be a right guy. You can eliminate the Smiths. Anyhow, God knows what would have happened to you if it hadn't been for Smith. Doesn't leave too big a field."

He grinned. "It's not likely to be Miss Grant, not from the way she looks at you. Or Munn, poor devil; it's a long time since he's done any running."

"Then it had to be Morris or one of the Lawrence party."

"Yup. But I'm not sure, in your position, I'd take a damned thing for granted." As other members of the party began drifting into the lobby, Swensen detached himself from the desk against which he had been propped, and went out.

It was Winifred's idea that they should all breakfast together and make the day a real jaunt, stopping at one o'clock for a picnic lunch she had ordered.

Both the Lawrences and Christie were at the big table in the middle of the dining room when Mr. Potter joined them, followed a few minutes later by the two young men and Janet. Winifred's manner toward Janet was so effusive that Mr. Potter wondered in some amusement whether she wanted to promote a marriage for her son. The woman was up to something but he couldn't imagine what it was. Unless, he thought suddenly, there's safety in numbers; with the whole party traveling together, Morris would have less opportunity to approach her.

The conducted tour was breakfasting on a wave of reminiscence about the mule trip, the women's voices high and shrill. The Smiths came in and Lawrence hailed them jovially.

"Join us, won't you? Probably we won't see you again and you're a nice young couple. Hope your honeymoon lasts forever, like Winifred's and mine."

Winifred gave her husband a sidelong look of intimate understanding and smiled. The display made Mr. Potter a trifle ill but it did not bother Lawrence. The latter went on in his self-appointed role of master of ceremonies.

"Where's that waiter? We'd like to get started in about half an hour. Of course, the most comfortable time to travel over the desert is at night but Winifred doesn't like night driving. Anyhow, we don't want Christie to miss anything."

His beaming smile faded as Morris came into the dining room and coolly joined the group at the big table.

"Morning, Winifred. Morning, everyone. Looks like a nice day for a drive. Not too hot."

"So far," Burgess said. "Just wait until we hit the desert. You haven't air conditioning in your car, have you?"

"You haven't a car," Damon reminded his cousin. "Not even a license."

As Albert Munn shuffled into the dining room, leaning on his stick, Janet nudged Mr. Potter whose back was to the door. He got up to pull out a chair for the older man. Seeing Winifred shrink away in a disgust she did not attempt to conceal from the man's disfigured face, Mr. Potter began to understand Dr. Holman's intense dislike for his sister-in-law. Molly Smith engaged Munn in lighthearted and unselfconscious talk and an unpleasant moment passed.

It was during breakfast that Mr. Potter began to notice how Munn and Morris watched each other. When one man spoke, the other was instantly alert. This morning Morris's veneer was badly cracked. For some reason he did not desire Munn's presence at Las Vegas and he made no attempt to conceal his annoyance. Now and then, Munn revealed an amusement that served as a goad to the gambler's irritability.

The big air-conditioned Cadillac was the first to leave, with Lawrence at the wheel, his wife beside him, and Christie in the back seat between the two young men. Mr. Potter wished that she did not look so much like a prisoner stationed between two guards.

Seeing his expression, Janet said quickly, "Nothing can happen to her, Hiram; not in the presence of four people. It's just not possible."

"It happened to Ponders. In any case, there's nothing I can do about it."

Morris followed in a cream-colored Pontiac, waving cheerfully as he drove off.

Munn insisted on sitting in the back seat of Mr. Potter's car.

"Shall I drive?" Janet asked.

"I'm not so stiff today. Later we can take turns, if you feel like it."

After a few minutes, Janet, who had been looking over her shoulder while she chatted with Munn, said in a tone of surprise, "Doesn't that red MG belong to the Smiths? They didn't say a word at breakfast, but they are right behind us."

"Somehow," Mr. Potter said, "I rather thought they might be." He grinned. "I'm beginning to have ideas about Smith."

Once more they followed the road along the south rim. As they passed the spot where Noah Ponders had plunged to his death, the wheel jerked in Mr. Potter's hands, steadying again. Janet looked at his set face, looked swiftly away. She turned and saw Munn clinging to the side arm with a kind of desperation. The man was genuinely terrified of being driven.

As the road sloped downward, a deer leaped across. Mr. Potter pressed his foot on the brake but the car continued to gain speed. The deer plunged to safety and Mr. Potter put the car in low gear, pulled on the emergency brake, turned the wheel in a sickening circle that checked the speed but brought them to a halt almost on the rim of the canyon.

Turning, he saw that his passenger had been flung off the seat and was crumpled on the floor of the car. With a screaming of brakes, the MG came to a halt behind them and Smith raced up to the Buick.

"You all right? What happened?"

"Brakes failed," Mr. Potter said grimly. He looked at Janet, colorless and silent, and turned to Munn. Smith flung open the back door and lifted the older man gently onto the seat. Mr. Potter handed him a flask of brandy from the glove compartment, which Smith rejected.

"Just let him rest for a while. No brandy. He's had the equivalent of a kick over the heart." He turned as his wife came running up. "Help them if you can, Molly. There's a garage at Cameron. I'll get a mechanic." In a moment the MG rocketed off.

In the back seat the two girls were trying to make Munn comfortable. "He'll be all right, I think," Molly said. "He doesn't seem to have broken anything. He was thrown on

the floor and he may be bruised. It's shock more than anything."

Munn managed his one-cornered smile. "Nobody's fault.
Anyhow, I wanted to go to Las Vegas; the risk was my
own."

What compulsion, Mr. Potter wondered, had been powerful enough to make this man undertake a three-hundred-
mile trip across the desert, a trip that he feared and
dreaded?

"You're from San Francisco, aren't you?"

"Visited there for a few weeks," Munn said.

The MG came back, followed by a wrecker. The mechanic finished checking and said, "No brake fluid. Looks
like someone has been having fun and games." When he
had made sure that the brakes were holding properly, he
drove off.

Smith stood beside Mr. Potter. "You seem to be letting
this become a habit."

"Lucky for me that you were just behind again."

"Wasn't it?" Smith gave him an innocent look and
climbed into the MG beside his wife.

There was silence in the Buick for a long time after they
were moving again. Then Mr. Potter stopped the car, and
got cold water out of his small ice chest. Unaccountably,
Munn seemed relaxed and at peace, his right hand lying
quiet on his knee. It was a strange reaction for a man who
had narrowly escaped death and who had begun the trip in
a frenzy of fear.

III

The Lawrence party and Morris had pulled their cars
into the meager and totally inadequate shade of three

dusty trees, remarkable only for the fact that they consti-
tuted the only shade within miles. Mr. Potter's Buick and
the little MG had to be content with the relentless, baking
sun.

Lawrence, beaming as usual, passed cans of ice-cold beer,
sandwiches, and fruit. There had been no indications of
surprise when the Buick drove up, but that was too much
to expect. They had been in sight for some time before
their arrival. Mr. Potter looked from one face to another,
wondering, "Which one?" He noticed with considerable interest that neither of the Smiths made any comment about
his brake failure.

It was Christie who looked at Munn and got out of the
cool Cadillac into the desert heat to put her finger on his
pulse.

"You shouldn't have tried to make this trip. It's too
much for you."

"That's what I told him in the first place," Morris said.

"I am a little tired," Munn admitted, "but I am glad I
came. Very glad."

Mr. Potter exchanged glances with Janet but it was impossible for them to talk. One can hardly go strolling
across a desert for private chat unless one is courting snakebite and sunstroke. Both of them were aware that a second
attempt had been made to kill him. And the killer, as Mr.
Potter was beginning to grasp with horror, was someone
who was willing to destroy harmless lives to attain his objective: the children and the unknown dead of the
Mourner crash; Munn and Janet, if it had not been for
sheer luck.

When they were on their way again, the cars still traveled in the same order, keeping a discreet sixty-mile speed
limit. Now and then they passed enormous tanks labeled,

WATER FOR CARS ONLY, a salutary reminder that, regardless of the vast open stretches, speed was not advisable if they did not want the radiator to boil over or tires to burst. Now and then, a big snake writhed across the road.

Munn broke the silence. "That nurse is a kind woman."

"Miss Christie? Yes, she is very nice."

After another long pause Munn said, "The brake failure was engineered, wasn't it?"

"Probably."

"Benedict the married man was right on the spot."

"Fortunately for us."

"Curious couple, the Smiths. This looks not like a nuptial."

Mr. Potter grinned. "Suspicious of Benedict? We owe him a lot."

"Oh, yes, of course. He said something about this being a habit. Has someone tried to kill you before, Mr. Potter?" When there was no answer, Munn insisted, "After all, I was one of the potential victims. It seems to me that I have a right to know. If I'm going to be killed, I'd at least like to know who is doing it."

Mr. Potter stopped the car to change places with Janet who took the wheel after a careful look at the road in case a snake had decided to cross it.

"How I hate rattlers!" she said vehemently.

"They're gentlemen," Mr. Potter assured her. "They always give fair warning." He turned in his seat so that he could see his passenger's face. "You have a right to know what this is all about." He described the attempt to push him over the rim of the canyon and how the ubiquitous bridegroom had summoned help in time.

Munn listened intently and Mr. Potter had the curious feeling that the lame man was checking the story against something he knew.

"Do you think Noah Ponders was pushed, too?"

"Yes." The answer was unequivocal.

"You have no idea who did it?"

"Obviously the possibilities are rather limited."

"Or why he was killed?" When Mr. Potter hesitated, Munn insisted, "Or why? In God's name, man, tell me about it."

"I don't think you need to be alarmed. It was I, not you, who was the intended victim, and after today I'll try to stay out of your vicinity." He added to Janet, "And yours. No, Mr. Munn, you are not involved in this thing in the least."

"Will you, for God's sake, tell me what is back of it?" In spite of the glaring light, Munn removed his dark glasses, trying desperately to read Mr. Potter's expression.

"What is involved," Mr. Potter told him slowly, "is the distribution of Jake Stendel's fortune. The estate hasn't been settled yet. Someone dislikes my interest in it. You see, this doesn't concern you. You're not in the least involved, except by sheer accident."

Munn laughed harshly. "Not involved! Good God, man, I'm Winifred's third husband, Damon Knox."

10

"I MUST SAY, Mr. Knox," Mr. Potter remarked with admirable restraint, "you live up to your reputation for dramatic effects." He began to laugh. "Unkind of me, of course, but I can't help understanding now why Mrs. Lawrence is so upset. Three husbands on hand at one time is a bit of a much of a muchness."

"She hasn't recognized me," Munn, or rather Knox, said. "I have changed beyond recognition."

Remembering the wedding picture, there was no possible reply. At length Mr. Potter managed to remark lightly, "Quite a coincidence, all of you meeting at Grand Canyon."

"Coincidence, hell! I've done everything in my power for weeks to see Winifred and have a talk with her. My God, I've got to talk to her! It's essential. That's why I came back to the United States. I followed her out to San Francisco but she absolutely refused to see me when I wrote and telephoned. Finally I called at Jake's house. She wasn't at home. She was never at home."

The right hand clenched and beat in a frenzy of frustration on the side rest. "Then I read that Jake was dead and they had all left for Las Vegas because of Winifred's nerves. I knew what that meant: at best, scenes and screaming; at worst, her malignant brooding while she figured out how life had disappointed her. There are lots of women like that, the ones who go on believing until they die that their dreams should come true, that life is unfair if the dreams don't materialize."

"It's not," Mr. Potter pointed out mildly, "an attitude that is confined to women. After all, the ability to realize that life is disappointing and still to accept it as good isn't particularly widespread, or, of course, easy to obtain."

There was a moment's silence before Knox spoke again. "Well, I didn't know what to do then. I can't get around and I can't drive. How was I to chase from place to place on the Strip? It seemed hopeless. When a paragraph appeared in a San Francisco paper, saying the Lawrences were coming here, I took a plane. But I've never been able to catch her alone."

"Are you sure she doesn't know who you are?"

"Positive. She'd never recognize me as the Damon Knox she knew. Not a chance. Then Morris put in an appearance. God damn him!"

"What do you know about him?"

"My predecessor, as he likes to put it." Knox had uncannily caught the very intonation of the gambler's voice. "Not very much. I suppose you know the general background. Winifred eloped with that mangy prince before she was eighteen and old Jake hit the roof. He wasn't going to support his daughter's gigolo. When the prince found out that was true, he let her get a divorce without making

116

trouble. I understand he never had much luck in the matrimonial sweepstakes. Well, there was a dustup in the papers. Jake's money and a title made an irresistible combination. So when she married Morris she was careful not to let her father know. Far as I discovered, old Jake never did learn about that marriage."

Mr. Potter had a curious impression that Knox was feeling his way. The marriage, he explained, had gone on the rocks before he met Winifred. Apparently Morris had found out that Stendel wasn't putting him on his pension list, either. And all they'd had in common was their passion for gambling. Next to indigent sons-in-law, gambling was Stendel's pet hate. It wasn't—that is—Knox was groping his way toward a tactful explanation—he hadn't broken up the marriage.

He'd been doing a picture in Mexico City and met Winifred at a party. They'd seen a bit of each other. Then she told him she was getting a divorce. Knox's surprisingly resonant voice broke off. They'd got married in New York. Jake had taken it in his stride. Knox was making a big income, plenty to support a wife. They'd gone on together for five years. She'd been happy, as happy as it was possible for her to be. Contentment wasn't in her. There had been bad patches when her nerves acted up. But on the whole—

There was a long silence while the car ate up the miles; long, empty miles of rough sterile ground where nothing bloomed, baking heat that dried the mouth and lips and skin.

Mr. Potter remembered the wedding picture. Winifred had been infatuated by Knox's good looks. She had obviously taken the actor in a trap of pity, or, perhaps, pleased vanity.

At length Knox said in a shaking voice, "Perhaps that

accident this morning was meant for me, after all. Morris knows who I am. I met him at Monte Carlo. He is blackmailing Winifred. He made that evident when he showed up at the canyon."

"Oh, yes. For some reason he has her in a cleft stick, but at least two people are fairly sure of what he is doing: Burgess Holman and your own son." Abruptly Mr. Potter exclaimed, "I'll be damned! That's what made Damon upset his drink the night we arrived. He recognized you."

"There's no trace left of the father he remembered," Knox said harshly. "It was that habit I have, tapping out a theme from the Beethoven Seventh, that gave me away. One of those compulsive things I can't seem to cure."

Mr. Potter nodded. "That night after Damon took a swing at Ponders he went out of the dining room whistling the theme. It tied in with the rhythm of the tapping so I suspected there might be an association between the two of you."

"Damon didn't know I was coming to America," Knox said quickly. "So far as he was aware, I was living somewhere in Europe. I never intended to have him see me like this."

"But he spent half the night in your room talking."

"Yes." Knox's face glowed with the memory. "It's a strange experience, meeting your only son as an adult, talking to him, man to man."

"That's why he hit Noah Ponders!" Janet exclaimed. "Because Noah took that picture of you."

"That's why. He has a temper but he's not—that was an impulsive act. Emotional. He'd never—my God, you don't think he'd have pushed that fellow over the rim!" There was frenzy in Knox's voice. "He had no reason for it. None at all. And he was in my room all evening when you had your accident. I can swear to that on any oath you like. Every minute. He knocked on my door and stood there grinning at me and said, 'Hello, Dad.' "

Mr. Potter was silent.

"You see"—Knox struggled to be calm, to marshal and present his thoughts convincingly—"Damon would never have touched your car, knowing that I was going to ride in it. Never. He engineered the whole thing, of course, to get me down to Las Vegas. He—we've always been very fond of each other."

"So that's why you relaxed after the brakes failed. Up to then you had been afraid that it was Damon who shoved Ponders over the rim."

"He wouldn't do that."

"Ponders kept insisting that he knew you. Is that true?"

It seemed curious to Janet, now as in the past, that people answered Mr. Potter's questions, however little authority he might have for asking them.

"He took a lot of pictures of me at one time. He was getting started while I was at my peak and he was doing publicity pictures of actors. That was a long time back, of course. Then, one day, three or four years ago, I saw a picture of me as I am now. I was sitting on a bench looking out over the Mediterranean. He'd taken it with only a quarter view of my face, the good side; I hadn't even known he was there. Study of a weary old man brooding. A twilight picture with me silhouetted against the sea. Very effective. I think he won first prize in some contest with it. I don't believe he guessed there was any connection between me and the Damon Knox of ten years ago. Who would?" He stirred restlessly, trying to ease his position. "Much longer?"

"Nearly there. Only another twenty miles."

"I'm perishing with thirst." Janet stopped the car so that Mr. Potter could pour more cold water. All three of them drank thirstily. When Mr. Potter took the wheel, Knox gave a long sigh of relief.

Janet turned to him, laughing. "Didn't you trust my driving? I've never had an accident."

"I don't trust any woman driver. Winifred was at the wheel when this happened to me."

There was a long silence and then Mr. Potter said, "Do you mean she divorced you because of that?"

Knox laughed. "She couldn't see a lot because of the bandages and the casts. But when she found out there wasn't much to be done to patch me up and make me presentable again, she wanted out."

"Someone ought to strangle that woman!" Janet said. "She's beastly."

"She is still fighting Helen," Knox said. "Her older sister was a truly beautiful woman. No man ever looked at Winifred when Helen was around, and Winifred couldn't bear it. In some ways, for all that fluttery manner, she has a lot of her father in her. A drive to be in first place. More than a drive, a kind of sickness. It has made her an unhappy, dissatisfied woman all her life because, of course, someone else always is first. She is an inveterate gambler. That's what drew her to Morris."

"Is that passion for gambling strong enough to draw her to Las Vegas even when he is there, even when it might hurt her chances of collecting her inheritance?"

"It's about the strongest passion in her life. Like most of her emotions, it's a sick thing."

"Does Morris know that she was responsible for crippling you?"

Knox took his time. "That night at Monte Carlo we

both had a lot to drink. I talked too much." He added, "So did he."

"And Damon?"

"I didn't see any point in making things worse. Don't make any mistake about it; I hate her guts. But she is his mother. He never forgave her for the divorce, though he supposed it was due to some infidelity on my part. Damon and I were always devoted to each other. We're alike in some ways. I think the boy has it in him to be a really good actor, better than I ever was, if he can keep from being typed."

"Or if he can make a start. Something gets in his way, doesn't it?"

"Yes, but what is it?"

He had a man working on it, Mr. Potter said. A good man. If there was anything to find he would turn it up.

"You've got your eye on Damon, haven't you?" There was alarm in Knox's voice.

"Jake Stendel was murdered, Knox; the night of his death someone left a glass in his room that contained traces of white arsenic."

"God Almighty!" After a long, shaken pause Knox asked, "What put you onto this, Potter? Who are you, anyhow? Is that engagement of yours to Miss Grant just a trumped-up affair to account for you being out here? Is that it?"

"I'm a man who can't seem to mind his own business," Mr. Potter said lightly. "It was Dr. Holman who told me the story. He was worried about Miss Christie's safety because she is the one who discovered the glass. As for my engagement to Miss Grant—"

"That sticks," Janet said firmly.

The love affair did not interest Knox. "Christie," he

said. "I can't understand it. Christie isn't the woman to cover up anything like murder."

"But she did, and, so far as I can make out, the only one of the lot she would bend over backwards to protect is your son. Another thing, it is my personal opinion that Noah Ponders was killed in mistake for the nurse."

"Oh—my—God!" Knox's hand began to beat its compulsive rhythm on the stick. "At least Winifred is out. She couldn't have tampered with your brakes. She was always a lousy driver and Damon says she hasn't been behind the wheel of a car in years. Probably that means since my crack-up."

"What do you know about her present husband?"

"I don't know anything about him. Too young for her, of course, but he seems all right. Matter of fact, it struck me as being a fairly successful marriage. Winifred likes to run things, she has to run things, but at the same time she loves being treated as though she were helpless. I'd say off-hand that Lawrence doesn't especially mind being run. Anyhow, Damon tells me he was away from San Francisco at the time old Jake died."

"What does your son think about his present step-father?"

Knox shrugged. "He knows his mother. There's always going to be someone, and at least Lawrence doesn't throw his weight around. Winifred is wildly in love with him." He added dryly, "I know the symptoms. But if anything goes wrong with her inheritance, he won't be around long. Not that I blame him for that. She's hell to live with. Anyhow, Damon takes him in his stride. One thing sticks out a mile. Morris is your man; he must be."

"Why?"

"I don't know," Knox said.

Mr. Potter was quite sure that he was lying. "Look here, Knox, I don't know what you've got up your sleeve but if you know anything that could make life easier and safer for Miss Christie, you're damned well going to tell it. If anything happens to her and you could have prevented it by speaking out, you're going to discover that up to now you've never known what trouble means."

Janet gave him a startled look. She had never heard that hard tone in his voice before.

At length Knox said, "What is Burgess Holman doing with this crowd? He and Damon hate each other's guts. Always have."

Mr. Potter made no comment. His silence finally goaded Knox into speech. "You know, Potter, a good case could be made out against Burgess. He's been right on the spot every time. He was in San Francisco when Jake died. He can drive a car, though his license has been revoked. He has been drinking more than he ever has in the past, according to Damon. Or acting drunk. He might have appeared a hell of a lot more intoxicated than he was, the night Ponders went over the rim."

"I've got my eye on Burgess. Anyone else you would like to throw to the wolves?"

Knox made no reply.

11

THEY CAME onto the Strip at Las Vegas in the late afternoon. It must, Mr. Potter thought, be one of the most preposterous sights in the world. In the middle of the desert there arises a glare of light. The Strip, ranging from great luxury hotels to garish and more blatant gambling houses, stands in the middle of nothing, surrounded by nothing, a wide-open town whose business and pleasure are gambling; where the clang of one-armed bandits, the rattle of dice, the shuffling of cards, the clatter of chips continue without intermission twenty-four hours a day.

The hotel at which the Lawrence party had their rooms was near the end of the Strip, away from the town. Mr. Potter turned into the mammoth parking lot and a boy ran forward to park the car while another came out for suitcases. When Knox had been eased out of the back seat, his stick was placed in his hand.

In the lobby Janet stopped short with an exclamation of surprise. "Well, here it is! I thought the gambling rooms would be upstairs, or at least out of the way somewhere, didn't you?"

Strictly speaking, there was no lobby at all. The huge room was nearly dark. There were lights only at the green baize tables where intent people played cards, placed counters, threw dice. From around the walls came the unceasing clang of the one-armed bandits, as people fed money into their maws. At one side, in a dim cocktail lounge, a three-piece combo played softly.

As Janet, Knox, and Mr. Potter followed a boy toward the desk, the outside door opened and the Smiths came in. They waved a cheerful greeting.

"By the way," Knox said, "I'm registering as Albert Munn. That's the way I want it."

"Your son knows who you are. Morris knows who you are. And," Mr. Potter's voice quickened, "Miss Christie knows who you are."

"That's impossible."

"When Ponders took that picture of you, and Damon hit him and went out of the dining room whistling that blasted theme of yours, Miss Christie knew. She was so rattled that she called Mrs. Lawrence Mrs. Knox."

"Well?"

"So far you haven't accomplished anything by hiding under a false name; why not use your own?"

"Three husbands, as you pointed out yourself, are rather excessive at one time. The reporters might get hold of it." When Mr. Potter made no comment Knox asked irritably, "What would be the point?"

"Something might happen."

"That's what I'm afraid of."

"Look here, Knox, right now we are stymied. There are times when a little shock treatment stirs things up."

"And you think they aren't stirred up enough?"

"I still believe it would be useful for you to come out in the open. After all, what are you afraid of?"

Knox shrugged. "If you say so. I've been used to myself for a long time, but I still don't relish having other people see what happened to Damon Knox. Winifred—"

"You think the shock will be too much for her?"

"Winifred," Knox said, and his tone was almost a snarl, "is going to love it!"

In his room Mr. Potter took a long, cold shower and changed to lighter-weight clothing. He poured himself some scotch and added ice cubes from the insulated bowl on the table. He looked at his watch. Four-thirty. Seven-thirty in New York. He made his routine call to Weston.

"I hope," the detective told him, "they are paying you for this service."

"What service?"

"All these testimonials to the efficiency of the hotel and the grandeur of the canyon you've sent me."

"You may find that handwriting useful. I sent the stuff just on the off chance."

"You sound rather fed up."

"They've tried it again." Mr. Potter explained the near accident caused by brake fluid having been drained from his car.

"What are you tangling with, man?" Weston was aghast.

"I wish to God I knew." Mr. Potter told him the identity of the man who called himself Albert Munn.

"I don't know what you hire me for."

"Another thing. Winifred caused the automobile accident in which Knox was crippled and disfigured for life. Then she divorced him."

"What is Knox's place in this puzzle? Money, do you

think, or revenge?"

"I don't imagine it is either one. He earned a lot during his active career and he seems to have an adequate if not lavish income. And though, as he says himself, he hates Winifred's guts, I don't think he's the revengeful type. It takes a lot of hate to last ten years. He doesn't care a damn about her, one way or another. This is something to do with his son. He's all wrapped up in the boy. And a lot more to do with his predecessor, Morris."

"You certainly like them complicated," Weston complained.

"Have you anything more on Damon?"

"Yeah. I finally pinned down an account executive at one of the advertising agencies. Very cagey at first. And you'll probably age ten years or go into bankruptcy when you see what it cost me to ply him with liquor. He said they had been getting anonymous letters about Damon Knox, suggesting that he was involved in subversive activities."

"You mean the boy was turned down on the strength of anonymous letters?" Mr. Potter was incredulous.

Weston laughed. "You do keep yourself sheltered from the more seamy sides of life! According to this guy, Madison Avenue is a sensitive industry."

"Sensitive. Well, that's one word for it, of course. So Damon is being blackballed without knowing the charges against him or having an opportunity to refute them."

"That's about the size of it."

"Could there be anything behind this rumor?"

"I haven't turned up anything," Weston said. "A rather timid excursion into mild liberalism while in college, but on the whole he follows the pattern you'd expect from Jake Stendel's grandson. I don't think he cares greatly where the money comes from as long as he gets some of it. The one thing he's ever shown genuine interest in is the stage. Why don't you try to pin the boy down, Potter? You might get him to talk."

"I might. And you might try out those handwriting samples on your account executive. Anything new at your end?"

"Lawrence has a clean record. Nothing wrong there."

"Try to check that alibi of his, will you, for the time of Stendel's death. He was supposed to be in Santa Barbara getting in on the ground floor of some new housing development."

"Okay. So far as I can learn, the second husband has never been in any trouble. He sticks to the places where gambling is legal." Weston's voice changed. "What's that?" There was a pause and then he said, "Hold on a minute, Potter."

Several minutes dragged on before there was any sound from the New York end of the line. Then the familiar voice of New York's handsomest lieutenant of homicide said, "Hello, Bird of Ill Omen."

"O'Toole!"

"Yeah. Your stooge Weston here came to me in a panic; thinks you're trying to get yourself killed. Not that, on sober reflection, I'm completely opposed to the idea, still there's no point in going to extremes. I checked with the authorities at Grand Canyon. Noah Ponders' body was found this morning. Completely smashed." There was a little silence. "Completely smashed," O'Toole repeated soberly. "For God's sake, watch yourself, Potter!"

An hour later Mr. Potter looked at the array of bottles and glasses on his table, checked the ice supply, and tipped the waiter. As the latter went out, Janet appeared at the door. In a black chiffon evening dress she was breathtaking. She came in and closed the door behind her. For a moment she looked at the bottles and glasses, then she said in perplexity, "What is this? A party?"

"Not exactly. I've asked all the suspects to call for a drink before dinner—but not together."

"Why should they come?"

"They'll be afraid not to," he said shortly.

"Is that why you asked me to be here on the dot of six?"

"I need you, Janet. I hate to ask it but I need your help and I don't want you to be seen."

"So that's why you insisted that I wear a black dress."

What he wanted, he explained, was to have her sit inside his darkened bedroom and watch.

"What for?"

"What are you drinking?"

"Scotch and water."

He dropped ice into two glasses, poured scotch, added water, gave her a glass. He picked up his own, looked around uncertainly, and then set it on a side table against the wall facing the bedroom door.

Her improbably long eyes widened. "What are you trying to do?" she said sharply.

"Make things happen."

"No, Hiram, no!" She set down her glass, put her hands on his shoulders. "You can't take an insane chance like that. You can't. One of these people we've been seeing every day is a killer so ruthless and vicious he doesn't mind whom he destroys in order to get his own way. I won't let you."

His hands covered hers. "Steady on, dear. Nothing is going to happen to me. But from now on we're playing with all the cards on the table. Face up. All I want you to do is to keep an eye on that glass in case my attention is distracted."

"Sometimes you are frightening."

"Do I frighten you?"

She moved instinctively closer to him and his arms gathered her to him. He kissed her, recapturing that incredible moment of months ago, which he had put so sternly behind him. This was the time to break away, firmly, collectedly, permanently. He kissed her again. Again.

There was a tap at the door. Janet caught up her glass and hastened into the bedroom, leaving the door ajar. Mr. Potter straightened his necktie, ran a hand over glass-smooth blond hair and, aware that he was rather breathless, went to admit the Smiths.

"Mr. Johnny-on-the-Spot," Mr. Potter said as he welcomed them. He glanced toward the bedroom door as he passed it but the chair he had prepared for Janet was back against the wall and she could not be seen.

When he had mixed martinis for them he grinned at Smith. "How'd you leave Roland Adams?" he inquired gently.

For once the debonair young man was taken aback. "Well, I'll be damned! How did I give myself away?"

"What set me wondering, even before I saw you, was that indestructible wedding streamer wrapped around a wheel. All the way from San Francisco."

Molly laughed. "If you knew the care we'd taken of that

streamer! We just wanted to make sure people would believe we were bride and groom. As we are, of course.
Only"—for a moment her lips tightened in mutiny and
then she smiled—"old R. A. isn't a man for sentiment.
When he knew Jack and I were being married he wanted us
to come here for our honeymoon. He offered to pay all our
expenses, which, of course, was lovely." She sounded a trifle
dubious about that. "But he was really making use of Jack
to do a job for him."

"You're a member of his legal firm, I take it," Mr. Potter said. "Junior partner?"

"Good God, no! Just a minor cog. If I work my heart
out, there's a bare chance that in another twenty years I'll
be about sixth man down. Of course, to be sixth man down
in Roland Adams's law firm is better than being second or
even top man in most of them."

"Remarkable man, I take it."

Jack Smith, who looked more relaxed and less angelic
now that his position was known, thought it over. "He's a
great lawyer. One of the truly great ones. To work for and
with him is a terrific experience."

"But?"

"Well, sometimes I find that justice unmitigated by
mercy is rather terrifying."

"Use each man according to his deserts? That's not law,
it's judgment."

"It's R. A.'s law," Jack told him grimly. "Logically, I
can't find a flaw in it but sometimes it makes me uneasy."

"I can see that it might."

"R. A. got a telephone call from Dr. Holman some time
ago, telling him Christie's story about the arsenic in the
glass in Stendel's bedroom. Later, Holman called again to
say that he had told you the whole thing and you were

going to Grand Canyon to keep an eye on Christie. For once the Old Man was fit to be tied. He doesn't like having matters taken out of his hands. I don't think anyone ever dared do it before. So he arranged for Molly and me to spend our honeymoon here."

"If he thought I couldn't protect Miss Christie by my own unaided efforts, he was probably right."

"You don't really grasp the essence of the Old Man," Jack told him. "He didn't send me here primarily to protect Christie. He sent me here to find out how much truth there was in her allegation that Stendel was murdered, and Dr. Holman's suspicion that Dr. Mourner was killed in an accident that had been engineered. My God, Potter, what kind of person is it who would sacrifice so many innocent lives to attain his objective or cover himself?"

"That's what has been borne in on me, over and over. Especially this morning when my car nearly went into the canyon." Mr. Potter moved across the room, lifted his glass, sipped from it, glanced into the bedroom. It appeared to be unoccupied. "How much do you—and Adams —know about this affair?"

"Not too much. We can't check Christie's story about the arsenic without visiting every chemist in San Francisco and that would raise a stink. Get her to tell you, will you, which one made the analysis? And even if we found him, of course, we wouldn't know whether someone else left the glass there or whether Christie arranged the evidence. No fingerprints. As the Old Man pointed out, she comes in for a big settlement; she might have been in a hurry for it, and set up a plan to throw the responsibility on someone else. But since I've met her I can't accept that."

"Neither can I," Molly said.

What he couldn't figure out, Jack said, was why the glass

had been left in Stendel's room; why, after the man was dead, hadn't it been removed?

"I'm beginning to get an idea about that," Mr. Potter told him, "and I don't like any part of it." He forestalled Jack's inevitable question. "So I take it you and your wife followed Christie outside when she left the hotel with Lawrence that first night; that you were trying to follow someone when I was pushed."

"No, that second time I wanted to talk to you without anyone knowing it. I thought it was time we pooled our information. If any. I trailed you, saw you standing at the rim, then—well, I told you all that before. Just the impression someone was near me—and then you yelled. Then running feet in the dark. I tore over to the rim and turned on my flashlight. There you were, hugging the cliff, with only inches between you and space."

Mr. Potter grinned. "I'm piling up quite a debt to you. So this morning—"

"I figured we'd better come along. Someone doesn't like you very much, Potter."

"How right you are."

"I'd hate to be in your shoes at this moment, man. I'd run screaming for help."

Aware that Janet was overhearing this conversation, Mr. Potter hastily changed the subject. "Have you come up with any useful ideas?"

Smith shrugged. "What it boils down to, almost inevitably, with Stendel's will still to be settled, is who profits? We haven't got a big list because we can eliminate anyone who wasn't at Grand Canyon. Winifred Lawrence, Damon Knox, Burgess Holman—these are the three chief legatees. For my money, every single one of them is scared by that damned clause in Stendel's will. And I might say that's the one thing he had his way about with the Old Man. Adams nearly had a stroke. Told him he was asking for trouble. Particularly because Winifred and the boys are Maybricks, and all the Maybricks have a screw loose somewhere. Playing with dynamite, that's what it was."

"There's Lawrence, of course," Mr. Potter pointed out, "who stands to profit by anything his wife gets. She may not be generous but she's twenty years older than her husband and she wants to keep him."

"Yes, that's why Molly and I were sauntering after him when he took Christie out for a look at the canyon—in the dark. Speaking of Christie, do you think Ponders' fall could have been sheer accident?"

Mr. Potter shook his head. Ponders had simply got in the way. Christie must have been the intended victim. He told about the finding of Noah's body, and Molly gave a little moan of horror. She'd said all along that someone had pushed her. Or pushed against her. They had all been standing very close together because there was so little room between the bus and the rim. The jolt she felt must have been the jar as Noah lost his balance and pitched forward.

"The nurse has got to be made to talk," Jack said.

She had talked, Mr. Potter told him. And? Nothing. She swore she didn't know who had put the poison in Stendel's drinking glass. She didn't believe Dr. Mourner had been deliberately killed. But she had told him one thing. Theodore Morris had been at Stendel's house on the day of his murder and it wasn't the first visit. He had been there before, but only during Lawrence's absences on business trips.

Jack nodded. Adams had already learned that Morris was in the vicinity. He had hit the roof when he learned that Winifred had been secretly married to him. Stendel had never known about it. He had an obsession on the subject of gambling. But the main point was that Winifred had married twice since she had divorced Morris. She was obviously infatuated with her young husband. So where did Morris come in, anyhow?

"I think he's been in the picture for a long time," Mr. Potter told him. "Both Burgess and Damon know him, which means that he keeps cropping up in Winifred's vicinity. And they both suspect, just as I do, that he has some real hold on her. He's blackmailing her." Mr. Potter grinned. "As you were listening that night, you must know that as well as I do."

Jack laughed. "Damn it, what are you, the invisible man?"

"Oh, there's one more thing. This Albert Munn—"

"I was going to ask you about him. He and Morris watch each other like cat and dog. Why did Damon maneuver you into bringing him down here?"

"Because,'" Mr. Potter said, "he's the boy's father, Damon Knox."

The honeymoon couple stared at him. "No," Molly said under her breath. "No! I remember his pictures when I was a kid. The handsomest man I ever saw. No!"

"What in God's name happened to him?" Jack asked, aghast.

"Winifred. She was driving the car in which he cracked up."

12

THE UNTOUCHED Manhattan remained on the end table beside Bertha Christie's chair. The big scrubbed hands were knotted together.

"So there it is," Mr. Potter concluded. "Except for the grace of God there would have been three more deaths this morning. How many murders will you take in your stride before you talk, Miss Christie?"

"You're positive the lack of brake fluid couldn't have been an accident?"

"Positive. And that makes it a lot more likely, doesn't it, that Dr. Mourner's brakes were tampered with. Three dead in that accident and two children maimed. This morning it would been Janet Grant and," his eyes held her startled ones, "Damon Knox senior."

She caught her breath, reached for the cocktail glass but her hand shook too much to hold it. "How did you guess?"

"Pretty much the way you did." He went on quickly, "You thought young Damon was guilty of killing his grandfather, didn't you?"

"No, I—" The shaking voice steadied. "Anyhow, Damon would never hurt his father." Color came back into her face. "Never."

His next question was unexpected. "Why did you refuse to take that freighter trip which Mrs. Lawrence offered you?"

"It wasn't like her. She isn't a generous woman. It—" Her hands twisted together again, then gripped the arms of her chair. "I was afraid it was blood money," she wailed. "I've been so worried. The only possibilities are Mrs. Lawrence, Damon, Burgess, Mr. Morris, Mr. Lawrence. And Mr. Lawrence was away. Damon—" She went on with more confidence, "But Damon loves his father."

"Miss Christie, you probably know as much about the Maybrick peculiarities as anyone. Just how peculiar are they?"

"I'm sorry, Mr. Potter. That comes under the heading of professional secrecy."

"We are dealing with murder," he told her, his voice hard. "Murder, Miss Christie. Ruthless, reckless, vicious—mad. Don't misunderstand me. If there is another death, you cannot divest yourself of responsibility."

She capitulated. "The Maybricks have a queer streak. One of the older generation was quite insane, I believe. Old Matthew, Mrs. Lawrence's grandfather, has eccentric ways, but there has never been anything more than that. His daughter, Mrs. Stendel, was a well-balanced woman, rather timid, but that was only because Mr. Stendel was such a dominating man. Her older daughter, Helen, Mrs. Holman, was lovely, serene, completely normal. Mrs. Lawrence is—"

"Don't," he implored her, "tell me about her nerves."

"She is moody and trying and selfish. She is unscrupu-
lous and she has to have what she wants when she wants it
or there is trouble."

"And the boys?"

"I don't know Burgess very well. I've never liked him.
He is surly and disagreeable and vain. But I don't really
know him."

"And Damon?"

Her face softened. "He was the most adorable baby and
always the sweetest child, with his father's wonderful
looks." She choked. "What happened to Mr. Knox?"

He told her grimly, watching her face. Then, to his
acute embarrassment, she put her hands over her face and
began to cry. He waited, moving from time to time toward
the side table where his glass stood, lifting it to his lips.

When she was quiet, and she contrived to pull herself
together quickly, he pressed her glass into her hand. She
drank from it, set it down.

"He was so—wonderful to look at. Handsomer even than
Damon is now." She added, "I've always loved Damon."

"And his father."

She looked up at him, color flooding her face, receding
again. "And his father."

She got up restlessly and walked around the room, pausing to look out of the window, to straighten flowers in a
bowl, to rearrange the bottles on the tray, to move an ash-
tray on the table where Mr. Potter had carelessly set his
drink.

When she had returned to her chair he walked over to
pick up his glass, swirled it, lifted it to his lips, spoke
abruptly. "How responsible was Knox for the breakup of
Mrs. Lawrence's marriage to Morris?"

"He wasn't!" she said harshly. "He wasn't. Mrs. Lawrence—Mrs. Morris she was then—was in Mexico. She sent for me because she was ill. Actually she had gone all to pieces because her marriage was already on the rocks. She had let Mr. Morris think that she had the Stendel money at her disposal. It was all she had to bait the hook."

There was hatred in her voice, and then she got herself under control again. "When he found out, he told her flatly that he was through. That's when she sent for me. Her nerves again. Then her father heard that she had been seen gambling in Mexico City and he telephoned her to return at once. Meanwhile she had met Mr. Knox and fallen for him. He—men are like children in some ways—was flattered by her infatuation and sorry for her, too, I think. Anyhow, we left Mexico and went to New York where she married Mr. Knox three months later."

"Where did she get the divorce from Morris?"

"That's where I thought, at the time, he behaved surprisingly well. She didn't dare stay out of the country after Mr. Stendel had sent for her and she was terrified that he would find out about her marriage to a gambler, so Morris said he'd get the divorce quietly and set her free."

There was a subtle change in Mr. Potter's voice. "So that's it!"

"That's what he has used to blackmail her with," Christie said bluntly. "He's been doing it ever since Mr. Stendel died. Her father would never have stood for that marriage, and if Mr. Adams knew about it he'd make real trouble for her."

"Ever since old Jake died." Mr. Potter was thoughtful. "But I gathered that Morris has been appearing in Winifred's vicinity for years."

"Well, they've run across each other, of course," Miss Christie said vaguely.

There was a tap on the door and Mr. Potter got up. "My next visitor. Thank you for coming, Miss Christie." He opened the door and she scuttled past Morris without a word. The latter turned to look after her, eyebrows raised. Then, with a curious wariness, he came into the room.

When Mr. Potter had mixed him a martini he went over to the side table where his own glass was waiting and lifted it in a salute. Tonight the gambler was once more the Man of Distinction, his suit excellently tailored, face bland and assured. Only that odd wariness clung to him as though he had walked into a trap.

"What the hell," he demanded, "did you mean by that crack about the ace of spades?"

"Murder, Morris. Murder." Mr. Potter drifted toward a chair near the window and Morris began to prowl around the room.

"I wondered," he said, "when Ponders fell. Something damned queer there. Only—how did you know it in advance?" He stood looking at the dark doorway beyond which Janet sat.

"I was speaking of the murder—murders—that have already been committed."

Morris finished his martini at a gulp, set his glass beside Mr. Potter's forgotten highball, turned around, his mouth slack. He gave the impression of a man completely stunned.

"What in hell's name are you talking about?" The veneer had gone again. This was the street boy reaching for his switchblade.

"Shall we take them in order?" Mr. Potter suggested

blandly. "First, we have Jake Stendel."

"Jake! He had a heart attack." Morris's manner was ugly. He moved toward the smaller man who watched his approach without stirring.

"Actually he was poisoned with white arsenic."

Something in Mr. Potter's voice stopped Morris in his tracks. His lips seemed to be out of control. Then he said hoarsely, "I don't believe it. What are you up to, Potter?"

"I intend to prevent any more killing. Stendel was only the first. Then, in a contrived accident, his physician was killed, as well as two innocent people. We come next to Noah Ponders, whose shattered body has just been found."

Morris sat down as though his legs had given way. Mr. Potter went to pick up the discarded martini glass and re-fill it. He pushed it toward his guest.

"What did you think of that business?"

"Someone jostled against me. I think you were right, that Ponders was pushed. But I swear to God I couldn't tell who did it. No one could. In the dark. But it's pretty obvious, isn't it? Damon had a down on the guy. Ponders probably had something on him and every one of them is itchy about the settlement of the will. Afraid something will come out to queer their chances." There was a gleam in his eyes and then he was passive but wary. Still wary.

"Damon," Mr. Potter said. "Somehow I can't see more than one killer here. That lets Damon out."

"Why?"

"Because this morning I nearly went into the canyon myself because of defective brakes. That was the second attack on me, as a matter of fact. And this time I had both Miss Grant and Knox senior with me."

"So he told you who he was."

"How did you happen to meet him?"

141

Morris shrugged. "I was playing the tables at Monte Carlo and this old wreck shuffled in." There was satisfaction in his tone. "He recognized me, of course. He'd seen me in Mexico when he was playing around with Winifred. That night I hit a losing streak and I was leaving the casino when Knox passed me and stumbled, dropping his stick. I picked it up and we talked for a few minutes. Then he asked me to have a drink with him. By that time I didn't have the price of a drink on me so, of course, I accepted."

"Of course."

Morris looked up quickly, reached for the martini. He and this deformed guy had had a couple of drinks—well, perhaps, three or four—and Morris had been grousing about his luck. He wasn't superstitious, he hastened to say, but no man could ride against his luck and his was way off. He'd got talking, the way you do after a few drinks, and he had mentioned his marriage to Winifred and how he had discovered that she had no money at her disposal, and how she'd left him and married the handsome actor, Damon Knox.

"And then, Potter," there was an odd expression on his face, "that guy with his shriveled leg and his useless hand and his twisted face looked at me and said, 'You don't know bad luck when you see it, friend. I am Damon Knox.' "

He mopped his forehead. "Worst shock I ever had. God, if you'd seen him in his prime! And Winifred had been at the wheel of the car when he was hurt. Well, after that, we sort of let down the bars. But I never saw him again. Next day I borrowed what I could and flew back to Mexico. Thought it might change my luck." He smiled maliciously. "It did, too!"

"That's when you started blackmailing Winifred, isn't it?"

Morris was out of his chair in a flash. Mr. Potter waved him back.

"At least four people know that as well as I do. Get off your high horse. You're playing a mug's game. Blackmail isn't a healthy sport and you're going to have a lot of explaining to do."

"Winifred won't make me any trouble," Morris said confidently.

"The police may. What were you doing at Stendel's house the day he died?"

"I wasn't near the place."

"Miss Christie saw you."

"She's lying to protect Damon. She has been head over heels in love with the boy's father ever since she first laid eyes on him in Mexico. And you know these middle-aged virgins when they fall in love." He smiled pleasantly. "Man, I'd like to know how she would feel if she knew what he's like now."

"She does know. Your game is played out. The sooner you recognize that fact the better."

Morris chuckled. "You're mistaken, Potter. You ought to get a gander at the hand I'm holding."

"I've seen your hole card."

Morris started, spilling his drink. He forced a laugh. "Like hell you have."

"Let's see if I can guess. You were unexpectedly generous about letting Winifred off easily so she wouldn't have trouble with her father or her inheritance. How did you put it? Oh, yes. 'She had it coming to her.' And twice you called her son a bastard." Mr. Potter leaned forward. "That's what you told Knox in Monte Carlo, wasn't it?

That you had settled your score with Winifred. You had never divorced her. That any time you wanted to you could pull her down on a bigamy charge. That Damon wasn't legitimate."

Morris managed a laugh. "You're quite a guy, Potter. Quite a guy. But just tell me one thing: I have it made with Winifred, so what reason would I have for killing anyone? All I have to do is sit back and put the screws on. Now you take Lawrence. He's the guy who loses when the story comes out. No wife. No inheritance. Think it over."

At the sound of a knock Mr. Potter went to admit Damon. Morris went out, pausing long enough to say, "Ask our pretty boy why he punched Noah Ponders. And don't let him tell you it was sheer youthful exuberance." He was laughing as he went down the corridor toward the elevator.

III

"So that's the story," Mr. Potter concluded.

From the time when he had begun to talk, Damon had paced the room, walking with the easy grace that was natural to him, his good-looking face haunted.

He refused a second drink. When he spoke at last, he said, "You're the man who stepped in when Eve Grant was killed, aren't you?" After another ruminative pause he asked abruptly, "Who got you into this business?"

"Dr. Holman."

For a moment Damon looked almost ugly. "Saving his precious son." He dismissed his cousin impatiently. "So Morris pulled a fast one on Mother. In a way I can't blame him. I know what she's like. She probably dangled the Stendel money before his eyes like a carrot before a don-

144

key. If he didn't like being tricked—well, who does? But at least I understand now why Dad has been so hellbent on seeing Mother. He wants to straighten things out for me."

"He didn't tell you then?"

He didn't tell me. He's a hell of a good guy, Mr. Potter. Not even bitter about losing his health and his looks and his profession."

The boy came back to sit down facing his host. "Now you've milked the venom out of Morris he can't bite again."

"Sure of that? At least he can rattle."

Damon laughed. "Oh, you mean that crack he made because I hit Ponders. Somehow I can't see Mother's Second as a defender of the underdog. That's not his line." His expressive face changed, filled with shock and incredulity. "My God, you don't think I shoved Ponders into the canyon! You can't think that. It's crazy."

"Crazy," Mr. Potter agreed quietly, and saw the sweat glisten on Damon's face. "What was that picture Ponders took of you?"

Damon blinked, taken aback by the unexpected question. "Oh, that! Raid on a club I went to. One of those things. We were all taken down to the hoosegow and booked for the night. Not of any importance. The picture was never published, you know." His amusement faded. "Mr. Potter, you're a sensible guy. You can't believe I'd try to kill Ponders over a little thing like that."

"The general impression is that Ponders was killed in mistake for Miss Christie."

"Christie! That's inconceivable. She's an absolute darling. There's not one of us who would hurt her little finger. There's no possible reason for hurting her."

"She removed the glass containing traces of arsenic."

145

While Damon was digesting this, Mr. Potter went on, "I have a certain personal interest in this affair, as you may recall. I've missed death twice by too damned narrow a margin."

"You can't believe I'd kill my own father!"

"Does your stepfather suffer from dizzy spells?"

"Good God, I don't know. According to Mother, he needs to be pampered like a lapdog, but he looks like a pretty healthy specimen to me."

The telephone rang and Mr. Potter scooped it up. "Yes? . . . Oh, Weston. . . . He recognized the handwriting on the anonymous letters. . . . Sure of that? . . . So it's Burgess Holman who prevented Damon from holding TV jobs? . . . Yes, it may be important. Thank you."

"What was that all about?" Damon demanded.

"You got the sense of it."

"You mean Burgess has been blocking me in my profession?"

"Burgess plus fear, plus, as I understand it, the sensitivity of the industry." Before Damon could comment, Mr. Potter asked, "Just how drunk was Burgess on that bus trip?"

"I don't know."

"And yet you assured Swede Swensen that you would be responsible for him."

At once Damon was on the defensive. "He was going to make a row. I thought it would be easier to let him go. I never—do you think he killed Ponders?"

"Why is your mother supporting him?"

"She isn't. He's just visiting us for a while."

"What do you think of him?"

"I never think of Burgess if I can avoid it."

"In my opinion," Burgess said critically from the doorway, "you didn't read that line well." He slammed the door and came shambling across the room. "You're not living up to your reputation for acumen, Mr. Potter. You should have seen me first."

13

Burgess finished his drink and, without waiting to be asked, went to pour more bourbon, add ice and water. His eyes were bloodshot. Already he was beginning to reveal the physical deterioration caused by his heavy drinking. The thick features lacked any suggestion of Stendel's power; they were like putty that had slipped a trifle, making them less clearly defined.

"That's quite a story," he said. "Sounds like Murder, Inc. Bodies to right of us, bodies to left of us. Now suppose you tell me what the hell business this is of yours."

"I came out here at the request of your father."

The unhealthy, blotchy color in Burgess's face faded. Mr. Potter's wayward mind groped for the name of the character whom Shakespeare had described as a "cream-faced loon." That fitted Burgess Holman at the moment.

"He's been riding me all my life. Why can't he lay off?" Unfortunately what he meant to be righteous indignation came out as whining. "Look, Potter, you don't know what it is to have a louse like that for a father. He makes as much a year as the President of the United States, but he won't even give me an allowance. He supported himself at my age and he never forgets it. He doesn't understand art so he won't help me get my opera performed. He rides me. He rides me! What's he trying to do, anyhow?"

"At this point," Mr. Potter told him without any particular sympathy, "he wants to know what, if anything, you had to do with your grandfather's murder."

"My—own—father!" Burgess slammed his glass on the table. "That shows you, doesn't it? Any normal, decent man would want to help his son. All he wants to do is to throw me to the wolves." He was working himself into a rage.

"Stop it!" Mr. Potter rapped out the words and Burgess was so surprised that he did so. "Where did the arsenic come from?"

"I've never seen any arsenic in my life. Christie is lying, Potter. Can't you see what's before your own nose? She wants to get me out of the way so her pretty little Damon can scoop my share. I don't believe there ever was a glass."

"There was a glass."

"Where is it now? You'll have to produce it, you know. You'd have to prove it ever was in Grandfather's room, that he ever drank out of it, that it killed him. Whatever Christie is trying to do, she's not going to cheat me out of my share of the Stendel money. That's straight."

"Where did you come across Morris?"

Burgess blinked at the change of subject. "He's been around for years. Always cropping up. Trying to get back into Aunt Winifred's good graces. What a chance!" He snorted in amusement. "From what I've heard, you're supposed to be smart." The thick lips curled in derision. "So

149

what happens? Instead of looking at things as they are, you're my father's obedient little stooge, playing his favorite game, pulling down Burgess. What about Damon, the idol of the ladies?"

"What about him?"

"Just keep looking, that's all. Something wrong there. He can't hold a job." Burgess finished his drink, got up to pour another, began to prowl, stopped to blink absently at the open bedroom door.

Mr. Potter lounged against the table, lighting a cigarette. "I won't have to look far, will I? A telephone call from New York just informed me that your handwriting has been identified as that of a writer of anonymous letters about your cousin."

"I don't know what you're talking about."

Mr. Potter's laugh whipped color into the pasty face as though it had been slapped. "You've made just about every kind of damned fool of yourself, Burgess. A stunt like that is not only vicious and cowardly but it's stupid. It backfires. For a man who wants to inherit some of the Stendel money you're building yourself quite a record. When Roland Adams hears of this last little trick he's going to wipe your name off the list of candidates so fast you won't know what has happened."

After a long thoughtful pause Burgess spoke quietly. In spite of the number of drinks he had consumed—and they weren't, Mr. Potter felt sure, the first he had had that day —he looked completely sober. "You won't do that," he said. "You won't cause me any trouble with Adams."

"Does Lawrence have dizzy spells?" Mr. Potter asked abruptly.

Burgess was taken aback. Then he grinned. "Darling James! When it suits him."

"What do you know about Albert Munn?"

The constant shift in subject confused Burgess. "Old Man Horrible? Never heard of him before. What's Damon up to, getting you to bring him down here?"

"He's Damon's father."

After an incredulous gasp Burgess let out a roar of laughter. "From Cary Grant to the Addams family!" It was Mr. Potter's expression that checked him. He stirred uncomfortably in his chair, discomfited by the other man's contempt and cold anger. "So what?" He was sullen. "Am I supposed to burst into tears because Knox had his pretty face spoiled for him?"

"Get out!" Mr. Potter's tone was like a whiplash. "And watch your step, you damned fool! You aren't playing with matches. You are playing with death."

Burgess got up, his thick lips working but no sound came out. Then with a shrug he swaggered across the room and the door closed behind him.

"He's vile," Janet said in a whisper from the darkened bedroom. "He's vile."

Mr. Potter started toward her, turned away with a warning gesture to open the door for the Lawrences.

Winifred had worked hard on her face but she had been unable to conceal the strain around her eyes, the tension of her throat muscles. A lime-green evening dress accented her bad color, revealed the ugliness of bones, the sharpness of shoulder blades, the sagging of breasts. She held a handkerchief and a small compact in a hand that was like a claw.

She came forward vivaciously, looked around in surprise. "Are we the first? What fun to have a little time to chat. Things have been so hectic the past few days we've hardly had a chance to become acquainted. . . . Oh, mar-

151

tini, please. And James prefers a Manhattan. How he can!"
She laughed, hurried on, fingers pleating the fabric of her
long skirt. "And where's your lovely Janet? I do congratulate you, Mr. Potter. In spite of all that money and her
good looks—and I've always insisted that she is quite good-
looking for that odd type—I was so afraid that no one
would dare to marry her. All that scandal about her
brother, you know."

"Winifred, my sweet," Lawrence intervened uneasily.

Mr. Potter grinned at him as he served the cocktails.
"Actually," he said mildly, "it's scandal that brought me
out here."

"People will forget," Winifred consoled him. "With all
that money—and one thing and another—though, of
course, Janet probably won't get back in the Social Register
—still—"

"Oh, not the Grant scandal," Mr. Potter said when her
voice had trailed off. "That ended when the crimes were
solved and the Grants were cleared. No, what brought me
out here was your father's murder."

"What are you talking about?" Winifred said. "My father died of a heart attack."

"He died of a dose of white arsenic."

At last Lawrence said, "You aren't serious, Potter? How
on earth could you be? His own physician issued a death
certificate and the body—that is, there's no possible evidence to justify such a statement."

"Miss Christie found a glass in Mr. Stendel's room containing traces of white arsenic. She had it analyzed. And
Dr. Mourner, who was, I understand, past the age of retirement, was killed when he left the house that morning."

Winifred gave a little shriek of protest. "No one would
do that. No one! Why didn't Christie tell me herself? If

152

there was any truth in it, she should have told me."

"She was afraid to tell anyone," Mr. Potter said. "You see, she wasn't sure which of you had done it. She didn't dare. And she was wise, as the event proved. Someone was trying to kill her when poor Ponders was pushed by mistake into the canyon."

Lawrence shook his head. "This doesn't make any sense at all, Potter. If Christie had been afraid of any of us, why did she come back when Winifred sent for her? Can't you see that makes nonsense of all these preposterous charges?" His voice was easy and relaxed. He might have been addressing a prosperous customer, plausible, reasonable, not in the least disturbed, after that first stunned shock.

"She came back, I think, because she couldn't rest until she knew the truth."

"You think," Lawrence repeated. "Really, Potter, I know you've done some remarkable things but this time you're way off the beam. Way off. And you're upsetting my wife. She's nervous and unusually sensitive and she should not be exposed to this kind of emotional strain."

Mr. Potter turned to Winifred. One of her hands gripped the compact, the other was pleating the folds of her skirt. "Please believe, Mrs. Lawrence, that I wouldn't be saying these things if they could be avoided. I know how shocking it must be for you to learn that your father was deliberately murdered. I do quite realize that this has been a trying situation for you."

She responded to the familiar stimulus like Pavlov's dog to a bell. "Trying! You can't imagine. One awful shock right after another. And my nerves are simply quivering. You phlegmatic, unimaginative people have no idea how I suffer."

"It must be difficult," he said sympathetically. "And on

153

top of all that emotional strain, you have the added embarrassment of three husbands on hand at the same time."

"Three?"

"Why, yes," he said, surprised. "Surely you know that the man who has been calling himself Albert Munn is actually your third husband, Damon Knox."

The heavily shadowed eyes surveyed him for a moment with blank disbelief. "Damon? But it can't be Damon. He is the handsomest—Damon looking like that!" A flicker of expression passed over her face, like a breeze over a pond. Slowly she began to smile. The look of malice and amusement grew. Her tongue licked out like a snake's. "Damon!"

"Your son didn't tell you, then?"

"You mean he recognized his father, even when he looks like that?"

"And Morris knows who he is. In fact, they met once at Monte Carlo."

Winifred stiffened. She clutched at Lawrence's hand. "James! James darling, get me out of here. My nerves can't stand it."

For once Lawrence was not responsive to his wife's demands. He was watching Mr. Potter closely. "What's this all about?"

"Jake Stendel's will, obviously."

"But what have Morris or Knox to do with that? They are out of Winifred's life."

"Are they?"

"What do you mean by that?"

"How long, Mrs. Lawrence, has Morris been blackmailing you?"

"Take me away." Winifred's voice rose hysterically.

"I can't let you go on like this," Lawrence said with unexpected quiet dignity. "You have no authority to treat my wife like this. There's no justification for it."

"Five dead people provide justification for a lot. By the way, how often do you have dizzy spells?"

Lawrence caught his breath. At length he swallowed, moistened his lips. "Occasionally. Nothing important. Heights bother me. Quite a lot of people are affected in the same way."

"Quite a lot," Mr. Potter agreed.

"I'm taking my wife out of here."

"Your wife?"

"Don't listen to him." Winifred's voice rose almost to a scream. "Come away, James. Come away at once. Don't listen."

"I suppose," Mr. Potter said, "you are aware that Morris never divorced your wife."

"James," Winifred said imploringly. "James darling, come with me."

"I've heard that you can be bad medicine, Potter," Lawrence said. "Be careful. Some day you may have to swallow a dose of it yourself."

"So I've often been warned. You realize, of course, that this is not a matter of personal intervention on my part. This is a police case. I would advise you to take it seriously."

Lawrence assured him that he was taking it seriously. He could see that it narrowed down. There weren't too many people involved: Winifred, who obviously couldn't hurt a fly; Damon, Burgess—

"You have an alibi, of course. Business in Santa Barbara."

"That's right." Lawrence sounded too hearty.

"Morris was in San Francisco when Stendel died," Mr. Potter told him helpfully. "And Knox."

155

"He hates me," Winifred said shrilly. "He'd do anything to hurt me. Why did he come here?"

"And upon my cue," Knox said as he came slowly across the room, leaning on his stick.

Winifred sat staring at him, her eyes absorbing in fascination the details of the scarred and twisted face, the useless hand, the dragging leg. And behind that look there was pure pleasure.

Lawrence was aware of it, too. He took her hand. "Come, Winifred. We're going now."

"But—"

"Now," he said firmly, and led her out of the room.

Knox eased himself into a chair and accepted the drink Mr. Potter offered him. "Winifred hasn't changed at all. Her own sweet self. I told you she'd love seeing me like this. At least she can be sure that no other woman would have me."

There was no possible reply to that. Knox smiled. "You want something of me, of course. What is it?"

"How well do you know your former brother-in-law, Dr. Holman?"

Knox was surprised. "Felix Holman," he said thoughtfully. "Not well. We didn't hit it off. He didn't think acting was a man's job." He was faintly amused. "And he didn't trust handsome men. It's all right for me to say that now when it no longer applies. He was a scientist. Art, whatever the form, was irrelevant. Trimming on the Christmas tree. Unnecessary."

"And his wife?"

"Helen." There was a fleeting tenderness on Knox's face. "She was a beautiful woman, Potter. And sweet. Perhaps not particularly understanding; she wasn't clever, but that didn't matter. You could talk to her without being judged, just accepted. Rare, isn't it?"

"Did Holman mind?"

"You mean that Helen and I were companionable? I don't know. I never gave it a thought. She was Holman's wife and I was married to Winifred. There was no question of any emotional involvement. None at all."

"Between a handsome man and a beautiful woman," Mr. Potter said lightly, "that is a most unusual situation."

II

The druggist, a strange expression on his face, beckoned Mr. Potter behind the counter into a small room at the back. He mopped his head. "I've never had anything like it in all my experience."

As he was still under thirty, Mr. Potter smiled gently. "I take it you found arsenic in that glass of scotch."

"I ought to report this."

"Of course. But first I wish you'd call Lieutenant O'Toole of the Homicide Division of the New York City police. I'll pay for the call. He'll know the proper procedure and take care of it for you. And ask him, please, to alert the local authorities. We're going to need them."

The druggist nodded, stared at Mr. Potter. "You'd better watch yourself."

"That's beginning to sound like a familiar old refrain." Mr. Potter left money for the analysis and for the New York call.

Janet was waiting in the Buick outside the drugstore. "Well?" she asked as Mr. Potter drove along the Strip.

"Arsenic," he said briefly. "You didn't see anyone stop at the table where I left my glass?"

"Every one of them did. Every single one."

"Well, that's that," he said philosophically. "It was just a chance."

"And now we haven't any way of proving which one of them did it. Oh, Hiram, I'm so sorry! I don't see how I could have missed it. I never took my eyes off that table."

By tacit consent they talked of other things during dinner while they watched a well-known musical comedy artist entertain, turning a somewhat weary charm on middle-aged women who responded with flattered delight. During the evening they drove from gambling house to gambling house, watching the repetition of the same scenes.

In time they felt that they were watching the same cast of characters. In each place there were the same gamblers, hot-eyed and tense. In each place there were the same well-dressed, unobtrusive young men who lurked in the background, watching with cold eyes to prevent argument and to preserve the peace. In each place there was the same impassive dealer of cards. In each place a noisy group worked indefatigably at the one-armed bandits, squealing when the bells rang and they hit the jackpot.

In each place Mr. Potter searched for the people who interested him. In time he saw them all. Winifred was at a card table, her face haggard, a highball beside her, while Lawrence in the background urged her anxiously to go back to the hotel and rest.

At another place Christie was, surprisingly, dressed in a modest evening gown, seated between Damon and his father, listening to a small combo. From a nearby table the Smiths waved and Mr. Potter caught Jack's eye. Janet, without being asked, gathered what was expected of her and went to take Jack's place and chatter with Molly while Mr. Potter talked quickly and the young lawyer listened and nodded his head, his eyes startled but alert.

"I'll have to check with Adams first, of course. But I'm pretty sure it will be all right. The Old Man is as impartial as an earthquake but he'd naturally prefer to see Stendel's family in the clear. If you are right, Morris—"

"Morris is the spanner in the works," Mr. Potter assured him. "If he's not actually guilty of the murders, he at least sparked the action."

There was nothing cherubic about Jack Smith now. He was a very troubled young man. "Damn it, I'm sorry, Potter. He's a smooth cookie, I know that. But he's not such a bad guy on the whole. And when you consider Winifred, there's a lot to be said for him."

"Famous last words. The Knoxes may not feel so charitable. Or Lawrence. At least, you won't have to keep an eye on Miss Christie from now on. The whole thing is out in the open and there would be no point in hurting her."

"So I take it you want me to transfer my attentions to Morris."

"And don't get sidetracked."

"Is it that serious?"

"It couldn't be more serious." Mr. Potter collected Janet and they drove on to another place where they found Morris so intent on his cards that he did not notice them. At a center table Burgess was shooting dice and making awkward passes at one of the briefly costumed girls who gave change for the one-armed bandits. He wasn't, apparently, making much headway with either occupation. The girl shook off his groping hand with a muttered phrase which brought color flooding his face. He looked up to see Janet and Mr. Potter close behind him, aware that they had observed the girl's disgusted rejection of his advances.

Mr. Potter turned away, tightening his grasp on Janet's arm.

159

"Hiram," she cried, "look out!"

He whirled to see Burgess with a glass in his hand, about to fling its contents into his face. One of the immaculate young men who remained so self-effacingly in the background, seized his arm, removed the glass, and eased him out of the room. It was as smooth and inconspicuous an operation as Mr. Potter had ever seen.

"Do you want any more of this?" he asked Janet. "If not, let's ride out on the desert, away from the noise and the bright lights. We have some unfinished business, you know."

14

THEY DROVE out of the parking lot, away from the town, its lights and restless movement, into the darkness and utter stillness of the desert. He stopped the car and turned purposefully to take her in his arms.

"Let me breathe," she protested at last.

"Why?" He barely lifted his lips from hers.

"I've forgotten why."

When he released her, he laughed rather shakily as he saw her hands go to her hair to straighten it.

"Hiram?"

"I love you." He held her gently this time, her head resting against his shoulder. In spite of the warm air she was shivering. "What is it?"

"Someone tried to kill you again tonight. That's the third time." Her voice broke treacherously. "The third time."

"That's why this shouldn't happen between us. I can't help getting involved in situations. Probably I'll always be involved. In some ways I'm dangerous to know, my darling. You had better reread your Donne: 'Take heed of loving me.' "

She released herself and turned to face him. Her voice was under control now. "You know what this is all about, don't you?"

"I think so."

"You know—who?"

"Yes."

"You aren't feeling very happy about it, are you?"

"Not very. Darling, I can't ask you to share a life like mine."

"Let's face it"—and he could hear the smile in her voice—"you haven't asked me. In spite of all my efforts! But I'll tell you this, Hiram Potter: you may not be a good insurance risk but you're the only matrimonial risk I'll ever consider."

"That being the case—" He switched off the lights.

It was dawn when he turned the car back toward Las Vegas. The comparative coolness of the night was already fading. As they came upon the Strip, lights were still burning, cars still moving restlessly from one gaming house to another; people in evening dress, in traveling clothes, in slacks and shorts, filled the darkened rooms, the lighted restaurants, in the town that never slept.

"It's like Times Square in the early morning," he said in distaste. "An untidy slut starting the day without bothering to wash or to take off her hair curlers."

"How much longer must we stay?" Janet asked.

"It's nearly over," he assured her.

Morris looked at his watch as he closed the bedroom door. Too late to go to bed; too early to get up. He slipped off his jacket, loosened his tie, and sat down at the small desk. Automatically, almost unthinkingly, he reached for a deck of cards and shuffled them.

The harsh light of early morning made him seem older than he was, older and more strained and, somehow, frightened.

With deft fingers he spread out a complicated game of solitaire and then stared at it unseeingly. Hell to pay. That's what it was. All this time there hadn't been a hitch until Potter poked his nose into the game. Morris let hatred rise in him, savoring it, tasting it. There were ways of dealing with men like Potter.

He got up to plug in a cord and heat a cup of water. As a man who was never sure of the turn of the cards, he had learned to prepare for financial shortages. As long as he could buy canned soup he wouldn't starve, at least. He measured instant coffee into the cup.

With the hot coffee came a sense of stability, of discretion. Potter meant trouble. He looked harmless enough but he was neither to be bullied nor bluffed. The man who tackled him would be wise to look ahead, to see what loopholes there were. Potter would slip through one like an eel.

What had put him onto it? Knox, of course, should not have been permitted to drive to Las Vegas with him. That had been asking for trouble. But what could he do, with Damon putting on the pressure, using all the slick charm that had been so useful to his father in the past. That would never again be useful to him.

Morris reached in his pocket, pulled out loose change, checked his billfold. God, the luck had run out on him tonight. In his suitcase he found his checkbook and opened it as though hoping that something might have happened since he saw it last. But the balance, of course, was still the same. Under two hundred dollars. Another night like this one and he'd have to hitch his way back to Mexico.

No, he'd be damned if he would. Play the game out. There was no real risk involved. He swept the cards together, noticed the one on top. The ace of spades. Once more he thought of Mr. Potter. He hesitated.

Then he snapped the cards together, put them back in their case. "It's a gamble," he admitted, "but what the hell!"

III

Winifred's frantic sobbing went on, sounding, Lawrence thought in exhaustion, like hiccups or the gobbling of a hen. He hadn't had a wink of sleep and he needed it. He was going to have to be clearheaded in the morning. If he knew the signs, the whole thing was going to explode in his face.

He tried to bury his face in the pillow, to muffle the hysterical crying. Damn the woman! Why couldn't she shut up and give him a chance to think? What was he going to do now? He had to make up his mind and make it up fast.

He slid out of bed and Winifred sat up abruptly.

"Where are you going?"

"I want a cigarette. Just a cigarette. Any objection?"

"James darling, don't sound like that. So cold. So like a stranger. Come back here. Just a minute."

He stood beside the bed, looking down at her face, swollen from crying, mascara streaked on her cheeks, her hair disheveled. God, but she was ugly! He shivered with distaste.

A hot, feverish hand groped for his, clutched it so hard her long nails bit into his skin.

"James, I love you. I'd rather die than lose you. Promise me that I'll never lose you."

Somehow he was too tired to discipline his face. He tried to release his hand but he could not do it without hurting her.

She stretched out her other hand, attempted to draw him down beside her. "Don't look at me like that," she implored. "Don't hurt your Winifred. Oh, darling, don't be cross."

Cross, he thought sardonically. Murder, blackmail, bigamy, and she says don't be cross.

"Won't you speak to me?"

He sat on the edge of the bed, looking with detachment at her ravaged face.

"Say something," she insisted.

"Was Potter telling the truth when he said you and Morris were never divorced?"

"That's a lie!" She strained upward toward him, the sheet dropping away, revealing the bony shoulders. In the cruel light of early morning, the sagging lines under her chin, the wrinkling of her throat were revealed. "Teddy is just trying to make trouble."

"At least," Lawrence said, watching her, "he's making money. What are you paying him for, Winifred?"

"He's hard up," she said quickly. "We parted in a friendly way, you know. It was just that Damon came along and swept me off my feet." Her expression changed.

"That revolting old man! I don't know what he told Mr. Potter but I'm pretty sure he's behind all this."

Lawrence's expression changed. "If that is true," he said slowly, "if he knows his son is illegitimate—"

Winifred whimpered at the word but he ignored it, released his hand with a jerk, went to stand at the window, his back to her.

"James?"

"What," he asked, his voice hard and direct, "is going to happen to us now?"

With that occasional shrewdness that always surprised him she said, "R. A. need never know anything about this; that is, if it's true Teddy tricked me about the divorce. I'll get one quietly somewhere and we can remarry."

He said nothing at all.

Ugly color crept up from her throat to her forehead. "The estate will be settled in a few months. We could go somewhere. That yacht you saw—remember?—and liked so much? I might give it to you for a new honeymoon trip."

It was a long time before he answered and he barely recognized his own voice. "And what will Damon do?"

"Which one?"

"Either—or both?"

IV

In the twin bed next to his father's, in the room into which he had moved over Winifred's protests, Damon looked wide-eyed at the ceiling. By the light, shallow breathing and the uneasy movements he knew that his father was wakeful, too.

"Asleep, Dad?" he asked in a low tone.

"No," Knox said in the voice that was so shockingly

alive in the withered body. "Anything wrong?"

Damon laughed softly. "At this point it would be hard to think of anything that isn't wrong."

Knox's hand reached above his head, tapped against the wall over the bed its incessant rhythm.

"God damn Morris! To have done that to you."

"Take it easy, Dad. If the truth comes out, he will lose a nice source of income. Anyhow, it's not all that important."

"Not important!"

"To be frank about it, I don't care a hoot. Do you know the percentage of kids who are born out of wedlock? It's enormous. The important thing is—"

"Well?" Knox said at last.

"After all, you are my father."

"And what are we going to do?"

"I have a couple of ideas."

It was a long time before the older man spoke again. "Damon," he said urgently, "don't be a fool!"

Damon laughed.

v

It was daybreak when Bertha Christie opened her eyes. For the first time in weeks she had slept deeply and tranquilly. If she had dreamed, there was no lurking memory of it. No shadow. No fear.

She got up, looked for a moment out of the window, picked up her robe and her portable radio and went into the bathroom. The sound of running water shut off any other noise. As she bathed, she found, to her surprise, that she was humming to herself the popular song that was being played on the radio.

Last night she had sat between the two people she most loved and had felt sure of their affection for her. The nightmare that had never left her since the morning when she had found Jake Stendel dead, removed the evidence of his last illness, and taken away the glass, was gone without a trace.

Mr. Knox needed a lot of care. A companion, perhaps, who would look after him. And Damon was all right. All right, she repeated firmly to herself. Why had she ever allowed herself to believe that he had killed his grandfather? She should have known better. She lay relaxing in the warm water. Whatever happened now did not concern her. It had nothing to do with her.

Unexpectedly she remembered Noah Ponders pitching over the rim of the canyon; she heard him scream. The soap slipped out of her hand. *That was meant for me. Meant for me.* I should have told them I broke the glass, she thought. That's all the evidence there was. I should have told them I broke it.

Movement rather than sound brought her head around with a jerk. She saw the hands that reached for the radio, that were lifting it toward the tub, toward the water.

She screamed, her voice muffled by the radio, by the thick walls, diving with all the agility of a body in fine condition toward those murderous hands.

VI

"It's nearly over," Mr. Potter had assured Janet. Nevertheless he was uneasy. There had been a time in his over-dominated boyhood when he had been racked with false anxieties. Times when he had gone downstairs at three in the morning to be sure he had not left the front-door key in the lock. Times when he had returned home from a party because he was tormented by the thought of having left a burning cigarette in his room and setting fire to the house. A constant bombardment of doubts about the things he might have forgotten, the mistakes he might have made.

Absurd as it was, he found himself now in the same dilemma. Everything was under control, he told himself firmly. All the holes had been stopped. Weston was taking care of the Santa Barbara end, Jack Smith would deal with Mexico. All the cards were on the table. But none of it helped. There was some factor he had overlooked.

I should have told them that Christie broke the glass, he thought. But if I had done that, they would know there's not a scrap of evidence. Not a scrap. There was no other way to handle it.

At length he gave up the struggle to sleep, got out of bed to turn on lights, pick up a cigarette and go over the case from the beginning. An hour later, he leaned back wearily in his chair, rubbing his tired eyes. He knew why and by whom the murders had been committed. He was reasonably sure that the nurse was no longer in any danger. Reasonably sure. But that wasn't good enough. Not half good enough.

There was no point in trying to go back to bed. Until he could get rid of the tension that tightened his nerves he would be unable to sleep. He disliked and distrusted intuition but there was no use in fighting it. The thing hadn't ended yet. Something was going to happen.

He yawned, looked at his watch, and called room service to order breakfast. While he waited, he showered and dressed. The scratches were fading from his face but there were, he noticed as he shaved, smears of lipstick around his mouth.

Something had come out of the whole ugly situation: Janet's love and a promise for the future. For the first time in his life his destiny was linked with that of someone else. It was a tremendous feeling. In a month they would be married and Janet was going to be there in the Gramercy Park house always, loyal and gay and beautiful, friend and companion and lover.

Anger stirred in him. This was the best thing that had ever happened to him and it should be a time for rejoicing, for planning. Instead, he paced his room, his nerves keyed up, waiting for something to happen.

15

Lawrence opened the door, saw Morris, and started to close it again. Morris threw his weight against it and walked in.

"It's about time we had a talk."

"Get out of here. My wife is ill."

Winifred lay motionless on the bed, terrified eyes fixed on Morris's face.

"She's not your wife," Morris told him coolly. "She's mine. You are o-u-t. The sooner you realize that, the better it will be for everyone."

Winifred whimpered and was still again, watching Morris as a bird watches a snake.

"Then you never got the divorce," Lawrence said slowly.

Morris chuckled. "I never got the divorce. Right now, Winifred is in the soup. If Adams finds out that she is a bigamist, she loses her share of the Stendel money."

"You—"

Morris stepped back as Lawrence raised his fist. Winifred jumped off the bed and ran toward them, grabbing Lawrence's arm.

"Wait," she said shrilly. "Don't do anything silly, James darling. We can fix things up somehow so R. A. won't ever know." She turned to Morris. "How much do you want?"

He smiled, pulled out a chair and seated himself comfortably. "Now that," he said, "is more like it."

II

The telephone in Mr. Potter's room rang as he finished breakfast.

"This is Weston. I've just talked to the Santa Barbara authorities. Lawrence was supposed to spend a couple of days at the house of a business colleague, who covered for him, thinking it was just one of those things. Now he knows it's murder he has changed his tune. Lawrence wasn't there."

"I'll be damned. Keep after it, will you?"

A few moments later, Jack Smith, no longer wide-eyed and ingenuous, but a quiet and alert young man, appeared at Mr. Potter's room.

"Look, Mr. Potter, this thing doesn't make any sense at all. We just got word from Mexico. Morris didn't divorce Winifred because he couldn't. He was already married to a woman named Cathy Binks. The police have been in touch with her. Seems they have been married for thirty-five years. She accepted Morris's arrangement with Winifred becQuse she thought he would be able to pull out in a couple of years at most with enough to keep them in clover. The police explained the facts of life to her, drove home the fact that this is a murder case. She says to urge

Morris to drop out of the game; the odds are against him."

"So that's it!"

Jack nodded. "Morris had his eyes on the jackpot. You know, I've never really seen a big gambler in operation before. How much do you suppose he's conned out of Winifred?"

"No idea. But when I think what he's done to Knox, what he tried to do to Damon—"

The telephone rang. The words were so jumbled that he could not make them out at all.

"Slow down," he said. "Now then, what has happened?"

There were confused voices and then Lawrence said, "That you, Potter? I think you'd better come along here."

"What's wrong?"

"It's Christie. She's—gone."

"Gone? Dead?"

"No, no. But we thought—better you than the police."

"Where are you now?"

"Our own room."

Mr. Potter did not wait for an elevator. Lawrence opened the door as soon as he knocked. He looked white and strained. Behind him Winifred lay on the bed, crying hysterically.

"What happened?"

"Winifred has been terribly upset. A while ago I tried to get Christie on the phone; I thought she might give the poor girl a massage or something to quiet her down because she's all worn out. There was no answer, so Winifred had me go up to Christie's room. I'd better show you."

They walked up a flight of stairs and along a hallway. Lawrence turned the knob of a door and opened it.

"Was this unlocked when you came here before?"

Lawrence nodded. Mr. Potter followed him into the

room. The bed was unmade, a nightgown lay across the foot. Lawrence pointed toward the open bathroom door but he stood back and did not attempt to go in.

The room was still steamy from a hot bath, soapy water filled the tub. The bath mat was soaking wet and several wet towels lay on it. In a corner of the room, as though it had been thrown there, was a small radio from which a voice was announcing, "You have just heard the latest news."

For a long time Mr. Potter looked around grimly. In the bedroom he asked, "Can you tell what clothes are gone?"

Lawrence shook his head. "Her suitcase is here; it looks as though she didn't pack anything. What on earth made her leave in such a hurry?"

"We don't know that she left of her own free will," Mr. Potter told him.

"You mean someone forced her to go?"

"We've got to find her, Lawrence. She's in danger."

"You didn't expect this development, did you?"

"Don't you think"—Mr. Potter was suddenly savage— "I'd have prevented it if I had guessed?"

Jack Smith, who was waiting in Mr. Potter's room, turned as the latter came in. "What happened?"

"All the evidence points to the fact that someone tried to electrocute Christie in her bath." Mr. Potter's expression stopped the exclamation on Jack's lips. The evidence, he went on to point out, could be misleading. Christie could have staged the whole setup. He agreed that it didn't seem probable.

"So she has either run away or she has been kidnaped. If she is still alive," Jack said.

There were too many watchful eyes, Mr. Potter reminded him, for it to be likely that anyone could smuggle a dead body out of the hotel. Everyone, of course, would be questioned: elevator men, maids, house detectives. O'Toole had probably been in touch with the local authorities and paved the way.

O'Toole had. But no one admitted to having seen Christie. She could, of course, have walked down the stairs and left the hotel unobserved. While Mr. Potter gave orders, Jack diligently checked with airplane and taxi companies, but it might be hours before there was anything definite, at least from the cabbies.

"This doesn't fit at all with your ideas, does it?"

"It doesn't fit anything," Mr. Potter said helplessly.

"How about the rest of the party? Can you eliminate any of them?"

Knox answered his telephone sleepily. At Mr. Potter's question he was wide awake.

"Christie? No, I haven't seen her since last evening. She and Damon and I had a couple of drinks together and talked, and then we left her in the lobby. She was going up to bed."

"Was she in good spirits?"

"The best," Knox said, and Mr. Potter believed him.

"I understand your son has moved to your room. Is he there?"

"He got up early and went down for breakfast. I'm a late sleeper."

"What time did Damon go out?"

"I don't know. I was asleep." Knox tried to hide his alarm. "What's wrong with Christie?"

"She has disappeared. I want to see Damon as soon as he shows up."

While Jack lighted one cigarette from another, Mr. Potter handled the telephone. No one answering the description of the nurse had taken a plane out of Las Vegas.

Burgess did not answer repeated calls on the telephone. Morris finally replied. He'd gone out for an early walk, which seemed highly improbable, and had had breakfast. Anything wrong? No, he hadn't noticed Miss Christie at all. Hadn't seen her all evening. She wasn't, he added with a chuckle, his type. Anything he could do, of course. Morris, obviously, was enjoying himself.

"I practically put Morris to bed last night," Jack said when the call ended. "I suppose I should have stayed outside his room. But it never occurred to me that he was dangerous, if you know what I mean."

Mr. Potter knew what he meant. He, too, had assumed Morris would be in danger. Blackmail was not a healthy occupation. He looked at his watch. There was still no reply from Burgess's room, and a maid reported that the place looked as though a first-class row had been going on, furniture knocked over, a lamp broken. There was no word from Damon, who could hardly spend three hours having breakfast.

Mr. Potter called Janet's room.

III

"Almost over," Janet thought as she undressed. For a few minutes she sat brushing her hair, seeing it shine in the light, aware of her own beauty and rejoicing in it. This, at least, she had to give Hiram Potter.

There was trouble ahead. Immediate trouble, certainly, before the ugly repercussions from Jake Stendel's murder could come to an end. She had not been fooled by Hiram's calm reassurance.

There would be problems like this after they were married. As long as he lived Hiram would stick his neck out, be caught in a web of curiosity, a net of compassion, unable to stay aloof from other people's problems.

At least she had had fair warning. She turned on her side, smiling. Whatever lay ahead, it would be interesting. And there would always be Hiram.

Somewhere a bell was ringing insistently. Janet opened her eyes, heard the shrill peal of the telephone, looked at her travel clock. It was only eight. She smiled. Hiram, of course.

She lifted the telephone, settled back comfortably on her pillows. "Good morning, darling."

"Janet?"

Her smile faded.

"Janet, this is Damon. I'm sorry to call you so early but I'm in a quandary."

"What's wrong?"

"Someone tried to kill Christie early this morning." As Janet gave an exclamation of horror he went on, "She got away. Scared out of her wits. Went into hiding. The whole place has been turned upside down hunting for her. Potter is out looking now. Well, I had a hunch and I've found her, only I don't know what is wrong. She says she won't come back. I think for some reason she's afraid of me."

"Of you!" Janet said in surprise. "But you've always been her favorite."

"I know, but there it is. If you'd come along, she would trust you."

"Where are you?"

Damon gave directions. "Darling James's car is in the parking lot with his keys in it. Do come as quickly as you can. The poor woman is hysterical."

Janet tumbled into her clothes, caught up her handbag

and rang for the elevator. Even now there were intent faces over the gambling tables in the lobby. The brilliant morning light made her blink and she groped for dark glasses, shook her head at the boy who came running up to get her car, walked along the immense parking lot until she saw Lawrence's big Cadillac.

It wasn't until she was at the wheel, until she had found the keys hanging so trustfully in the lock, that she was fully awake, that she began to wonder. Both of the Lawrences were careful of their possessions. Darling James, he had said. But it wasn't Damon who called Lawrence that; it was Burgess.

And Burgess was climbing into the seat beside her. Burgess with, unbelievably, a revolver in his hand. Burgess with one eye swollen shut and as black as though he had made up for a slapstick comedy, his thick lips cut, his face marked from a terrible beating.

Her first feeling was one of sheer surprise and then indignation. "If this is your idea of a joke," she began angrily.

"No joke. This little thing is loaded."

"Then you're crazy," she declared, saw his expression and suddenly she was afraid.

"Don't," he said softly, in the voice which was so like Damon's, "ever say that again. Ever."

Her hand moved toward the horn.

"Don't touch that. Back out and go where I tell you. If you try to attract any attention I'll kill you now. If this stunt doesn't come off I haven't anything to lose, so you had better make sure it does."

For a moment she was so paralyzed with fear that she could not move. He seemed aware of the fact and waited until she had taken a long breath, steadied herself.

"Now start the car and do as you are told."

"What are you trying to prove?" she asked, her voice shaking. "Do you think you can kidnap me and get away with it?"

"I'm holding you as a hostage," he said in his lazy voice.

"But why?"

"Because your friend Potter won't do anything to injure you. We're going to hole up for a while until he agrees to my terms."

"Then all that about Christie—"

"Oh, she got away all right. And she still has the glass. That's the only evidence. The only scrap of evidence. But Potter can keep her quiet about it. He'll meet my terms because he will have to."

"If you think," she said, trying to speak coolly, "for one single minute that Hiram will let you get away with murder you're—" She broke off.

Out of your mind. She had to be careful. She didn't know Burgess in this mood. She mustn't make a slip like that again.

"Get this straight, Janet. Any slipup, any attempt to play it cute, and you've had it. When we find a nice private telephone, you're going to call Potter. You're going to tell him to get in touch with Roland Adams and say that everything is on the up and up. And he'd better make Adams believe he's telling the truth."

"Then what?"

"Then you'll stay with me until Adams winds up the estate. After that, you can go to hell so far as I am concerned."

Stay with him. Stay with Burgess. Surely he wasn't mad enough to think he could get away with it. But he was that mad. In his present mood there was no point in arguing with him. He wasn't reasonable enough to understand that his plan had no chance of succeeding, that Hiram would get in touch with Adams once she was safe.

Once she was safe. Whatever happened, it wasn't likely that she would remain alive after she called Hiram. Not if Burgess had killed his grandfather and the others. All the others.

She drove as slowly as possible, trying not to notice the revolver clutched in his fist. She stole a quick look at him, saw the small eyes filled with hate, one of them almost closed by that grotesque black swelling.

They were out of town now, on the desert with its relentless light, its relentless heat. She rolled down the window and Burgess said sharply, "Close it!" He told her how to turn on the air conditioning.

"Where are you taking me?" she asked at length.

"You'll find out." As he bent his head to light a cigarette she looked at him. He was blustering. He had no plan. He didn't know where to take her.

"Turn off here," he said, and she left the highway for a dirt road, already half overgrown. Her heart sank at leaving the main road.

"Hiram will find us, you know," she said with more confidence than she felt.

She was aware of the bitter hatred that corroded him, of the lonely hostility of that grotesque figure beside her. For the first time she wondered what it had been like, seeing his own ugliness every day, aware of his cousin's good looks and relaxed charm, conscious of the unstable emotional strain of the Maybricks. To her surprise she found that she was sorry for him.

"Burgess," she said gently, "let's go back and be sensible. You'd be taken care of, you know."

"I'm not crazy! I'm not crazy!" The hand holding the revolver shook and she was aware of how close she had come to death.

After a long time she asked, "Why did you poison your grandfather? Why did you try to poison Hiram?"

"So he nearly got it." Burgess laughed. "Well, I'll be damned."

"As though you didn't know."

"I didn't know. And for your information—and I don't give a hoot in hell whether you believe me or not—I didn't poison old Jake. I've never even seen any arsenic in my life."

The curious thing was that she believed for once in his life, Burgess was telling the truth.

16

DAMON'S FACE had an odd appearance, a curiously blurred quality that, for the first time, gave him a slight resemblance to Burgess Holman. Mr. Potter saw that he had taken a bad beating and that either he or his father had done a professional job in an attempt to conceal the damage.

"Dad says you want to see me. Something about Christie."

Mr. Potter's brows arched. "What happened to you?"

"I beat hell out of Burgess," Damon said in a tone of savage satisfaction.

"And what happened to him?"

"I knocked him out."

Then what did you do with him?"

Damon's eyes flickered. "I left him there on the floor. He wasn't badly hurt, just knocked out, and a real shiner." His voice sharpened. "I swear to God I left him there. What has he got to do with Christie?"

"I don't know. They're both missing. From the appearance of her bathroom, I'd say offhand that someone tried to electrocute her by throwing a small radio into her bathtub. Whether she escaped in a panic or was taken away by force I don't know. It's anyone's guess right now."

"Christie!" Damon said in fury. "If Burgess hurt her I'll kill him."

"There has been enough killing."

"But Christie—why would anyone hurt her?"

"Because she took that glass out of your grandfather's room." He reached out to silence the telephone.

"This is Burgess Holman," said the voice at the other end of the line. "I thought I'd spell it out for you. I have Janet Grant. You'll inform Adams that everything is all right, and forget whatever you dug up on me, or you won't see her again. Is that clear?"

"You're lying."

Burgess laughed. "He doesn't believe me, Janet. You can speak to him yourself. But no tricks."

He heard her voice. "Hiram? He is quite mad. You can't let him go on, whatever happens to me."

"Where are you?" When she made no reply he said desperately, "Leave the receiver off if you possibly can. Janet!"

There was a curious dry sound he could not identify, then he heard her scream once. There was a shot that echoed and re-echoed in his ear.

II

They had driven for over an hour when she looked at the gas gauge. It was registering nearly empty. Her first emotion was the annoyance of any driver; then her eyes widened with pleased surprise.

"What are you grinning about?" Burgess demanded.

She could not keep the relief and amusement out of her voice. "We're practically out of gas."

Burgess muttered an oath, checked the gas gauge, told her to stop the car. "Darling James keeps extra gas for emergencies. Don't open the door or I'll let you have it."

She heard him moving things in the trunk, heard the top slam down. He got back in beside her and his expression of mingled frustration and fury conquered any desire she had to laugh.

"Go on," he said.

The car, heavy as it was, jolted over the rough dirt road. There was nothing moving in the landscape except for an occasional bird of prey hovering overhead. She shivered. The road curved around a mound and he let out an exclamation.

"Draw up at that gas station."

There actually was a gas station, but a sign on the door read: CLOSED UNTIL MAY 1. Burgess stared at it in dismay. Then his eyes moved on to a public telephone booth. He grinned and got out of the car. "Come along."

Feeling the metal prod her back, Janet stumbled ahead of him. It would take so little, in his state of tension, to make him pull the trigger. And never before had she known how much she wanted to live, with everything opening out for her. She had always known in some part of her heart that she would never marry Hiram Potter. But she had never guessed that it would end like this, shot like a dog on this forsaken desert, left to bleach in the sun.

Even in her momentary expectation of a shot, she was still subconsciously aware of snakes, watching the dirt road carefully for anything that moved.

Burgess crowded her into the baking booth beside him.

The glass was hot enough to blister her skin as she was pressed against it. The temperature in here must be over a hundred and twenty, she thought.

She heard Burgess speak, only half aware of his words, conscious that at the other end of the line were Hiram and sanity and safety. Hiram would never give up; he would never surrender to this blackmail. Or—perhaps he would. Remembering the words he had whispered to her last night, she knew that this might be his breaking point. He would call Roland Adams, assure him that Stendel's death had been natural.

But it didn't make sense. There was nothing to prevent him from telling the truth when she was safe. When she was safe.

Burgess thrust the telephone, wet from his hand, into her own. She heard the voice she loved.

"Hiram?" she said, without having planned it. "He is quite mad. You can't let him go on, whatever happens to me."

"Where are you?" he demanded.

She looked around in despair. How could she describe a forsaken road leading to nowhere in this strange, rough desert? She looked down, her eyes widening with horror, and Burgess followed her gaze to the thick snake crawling across the road.

"Leave the receiver off if you possibly can," she heard Hiram say. "Janet!"

Her eyes were still on the snake. It was almost at the booth. It coiled, rattled, struck at Burgess's leg. She screamed as he leaped aside and shot, blowing the rattler's head off.

While the headless body writhed on the ground as though it maintained some unspeakable life of its own,

Burgess seized her hand; his face was convulsed.

"Back in the car," he said hoarsely.

She let him drag her away from the booth into the cool safety of the car. Behind her the telephone dangled on its cord.

III

This time Burgess took the wheel with Janet beside him. The road had petered out. He drove on slowly and aimlessly until the motor sputtered, stopped. They had not gone half a mile from the telephone booth. After passing a deserted shack, which was falling apart, they had seen nothing but the desert itself. The frenzy that had driven Burgess seemed to have drained out of him. His mouth was slack. His hands dropped from the wheel.

"Well, that's that," he said flatly.

"What happens now?"

"We wait."

She opened the door on her side. Without moving, he said in his lazy voice, "Every week people are brought into Las Vegas. People who won't wait in their cars for help, so they die. Sunstroke, snakebite, mountain lions or whatever they have out here. Anyhow, if you leave the car you'll die."

His lower lip, dried by the heat, cracked by the beating he had taken from Damon, began to bleed and he dabbed at it automatically with his handkerchief.

"Don't use that," Janet said in horror. "It's filthy. You'll get an infection. Here, take mine."

Unexpectedly, he began to laugh. "Janet, you're wonderful." For the first time he sounded like himself.

"Burgess," she said impulsively, "you're in an awful

jam. Hiram is bound to find us, you know."

"How?" he asked mockingly. He looked around at un-marked desert.

"He'll never give up. Never. Sooner or later, he will find us. Your only chance is to surrender quietly when the time comes."

"They'll get me," Burgess said, as though he no longer cared. "But not until you are dead."

"But why, Burgess? Why?"

He smiled at her lazily, as though he were too tired for anger. "Why not? I've been crazy about you from the first time I saw you but you couldn't bother to give me the time of day. Remember the dance where someone saw me with you—the only time you ever danced with me, remember?—and called out, 'Look at beauty and the beast'? Then Damon cut in. Pretty-boy Damon. You hated dancing with me, didn't you? Hated being near me. You know the kind of girls who dance with me? The wall-flowers at parties or the kind you never met in your life. Because I could pay.

"You never saw my beautiful mother look at me, won-dering how she had hatched such an ugly duckling. You never heard my father ride me because I didn't try hard enough to—and I quote—get full value from my college education. He'd worked his way through, with honors, and he never let me forget it. What the hell!"

He lighted a cigarette and then crushed it out in the ash-tray. His hand was shaking. Something in the atmosphere warned her even before he reached for her, dragging her into his arms, forcing her mouth open with his lips. She could feel a trickle of blood from his cut lip on her mouth and a wave of nausea swept over her.

He held her back to look in her face and she managed by

an immense effort to keep her expression impassive. She said gently, "How did you get yourself into this mess, Burgess?"

In his uncertain mood the unexpected note of sympathy sidetracked him. "I figured the only chance a guy like me has is to be in the money. Then old Jake came out with that damned will. I knew if he found out about my troubles in college he'd drop me at once. He was that kind of guy. And then—things happened." There was caution in his voice now; he was wary.

"What happened?"

"I don't know how much Potter found out. Morris never did divorce Aunt Winifred. He's been bleeding her white about it and she didn't dare take steps for fear her father or R. A. would trace them. And it turns out that Damon is a bastard." He rolled the word lovingly over his tongue. "So then—well, the idea sort of came up."

"The idea of killing your grandfather?" Janet was surprised to hear how matter-of-fact her voice sounded.

"Yeah. Once he was out of the way, the heat would be off, in a manner of speaking. Well, I didn't say yes and I didn't say no. But I took the matter under consideration." The familiar note of lazy mockery was back again. "Only I wasn't going to take the rap for it if there was any trouble. So when I found out what had happened to Jake, I put the glass back in his bedroom."

"You put it back," she said, bewildered.

"I was drunk as a coot and scared silly. I knew I'd be blamed if anything came out. I just grabbed the damned thing and then, I don't know why—partly because I wanted to see for myself—I went into Grandfather's room. He was dead and the place was a mess. I put down the glass and cleared out."

"But—"

"I don't know why," he shouted. "I just wanted to get away from there. Then Christie took the damned thing away again. God knows what she did with it, aside from having it analyzed. So now it's my word against—oh, hell!"

"Is that why you tried to push Christie into the canyon?"

"That's why. You know," he added plaintively, "I've had the rottenest luck!"

"So," she said, her voice shaking in spite of her effort at control, "did Noah Ponders."

"Yeah. Well"—he dismissed Ponders—"too bad, but that's the way the cookie crumbles."

"You're the one who tampered with the brakes on Dr. Mourner's car."

"Well, I got back to my room after I found Grandfather dead and I was sick. Then I heard the excitement in the house and Dr. Mourner came. I didn't know Christie had cleared things up. I figured he would tell them it was murder; we wouldn't have wanted that, you know," he said reasonably.

"But I don't see—"

"I was off my head!" Unexpectedly he shouted, "I didn't say that!"

Janet dared not move. This was like sitting beside a live bomb, not knowing what would set it off. There was a curious sound and she looked up. Another big bird was overhead. No, it was a helicopter. It dropped lower and lower, hovering over them.

"So they've found us. Well, I guess it's now or never." With his left hand Burgess drew her to him and with his right he tore her blouse down from the neck.

17

JACK SMITH started to speak, looked at Mr. Potter's set face, and was silent. Only the lines at the corners of his mouth betrayed what he was feeling, the tension under which he was operating. He went on steadily making telephone calls, his voice even, scrawling methodical notes on a pad beside the telephone.

Molly, coming quietly into the room, took one look at him and then went to her husband, her hand groping for his.

A waiter put down a tray holding a coffeepot, cups and saucers, taking a quick, curious look around him as he did so. There was always excitement at Las Vegas but not this kind. When it hit the papers, the big boys were going to flip their lids. Kidnaping! They weren't going to like that at all, especially the one who had got his daughter into a good girls' college. From now on he wanted respectability.

Molly poured a cup of coffee and pushed it silently toward the man at the telephone. He reached for it and smiled at her.

"I don't see what I could have overlooked. They won't be able to take a plane. Anyhow, Burgess has Lawrence's car. The state troopers are looking for it, setting up road-blocks. They've called out a helicopter."

For a moment the three of them thought bleakly of end-less miles of desert, of a car that, from the air, would look like countless others.

"If she was able to leave the telephone off the hook," Mr. Potter said, "it may help find the spot from which they telephoned. More delay, of course."

He remembered the queer, unidentifiable sound he had heard, Janet's scream, the shot. Perhaps she was dead now. All that time he had wasted, afraid to commit himself wholly to another person. And now she might be dead.

The telephone rang and he picked it up. He made notes.

"They've found the booth. It's beside a garage to the northeast of Las Vegas."

The telephone bell shrilled again. "What?" he said ex-plosively. "Are they sure? . . . No, I realize that. . . . No, for God's sake, warn the troopers not to get too close. If she's—still alive, that might provide the finishing touch. I'm going along."

He stood up, took the automatic out of the drawer of the table. "Where is everyone right now?" he asked.

"They are all in their rooms and there are men on guard outside."

"Good. See you later."

"Wait, Potter, I'm going with you."

"If she's still all right, I'll have a chance by myself. I don't dare risk taking you along, Jack."

"I'll lie low in the back of your car."

Molly made a small sound, was quiet again. Her husband gave her a quick, reassuring smile.

Mr. Potter studied his face and nodded. He handed over the automatic. "You keep this and cover me if it's necessary."

With Jack beside him, he pulled out of the parking lot, turned onto the highway, threaded his way through traffic. Beyond the limits of the town the Buick picked up speed, but even now, under stress, it was kept at an even sixty. This was no time to court car trouble.

Mr. Potter's hands were steady on the wheel, his face was unrevealing, but his thoughts were frantic. Too late. Too late. The scream and the shot had been final enough. But even so, it was hard to eliminate hope. What baffled him was why Lawrence's car—if it was Lawrence's car—had gone off the road onto the desert. What was happening?

The windows were rolled nearly to the top and an air vent was opened, to provide as much circulation of air and as little heat as possible. But still the temperature was almost unbearable. Jack moistened dry lips, started to suggest that they stop for cold water from the ice chest, changed his mind.

The road peeled away endlessly under the tires; the glare, even with dark glasses, half blinded them. Once they saw a big bird hovering almost motionless in the air and Jack shivered.

Then there was a quick blare of the horn, which startled him, and he saw the radio antenna of the unmarked car ahead of them. Mr. Potter pulled up beside it.

The man at the wheel nodded. They had been told that Mr. Potter wanted to approach the car alone. This was where he was to turn off. The telephone booth was only a few miles away, and another police car was waiting there for further orders. The helicopter reported the Cadillac had stalled less than half a mile beyond the booth. There had been no signs of movement in the car. No one had gotten out.

"Tell them not to move in yet," Mr. Potter said. "There's still a chance—"

The driver saw his eyes and nodded. Poor devil. Not that there was a hope.

"He's armed. Lawrence reports that he took a revolver belonging to him."

"I'll be careful. Very careful."

But not for himself, the trooper realized. For the girl.

The dirt road moved over rough hillocks, through desert. Mr. Potter saw the helicopter hovering. It rose like an overfed bird and began to circle. Then it was hovering again.

The garage and telephone booth came into sight. Again Mr. Potter pulled up.

No one had showed, the trooper told him. According to the guy in the helicopter the car seemed to be abandoned. Maybe the damned fool had tried to make a run for it on foot. If so, they'd find him in time but, this distance from water or shelter, he'd have had it. No, so far they hadn't caught sight of anyone on foot.

Mr. Potter nodded, his face set. If Burgess had left the car, it meant that Janet was dead. There couldn't be any other reason.

"Don't get into sight until you hear from us," he said. "We'll sound the horn if we need you. Get in back, Jack, and keep down, for God's sake."

When the younger man had scrambled over the seat and crouched on the floor, Mr. Potter drove on, traveling more slowly now. The road had faded out entirely but the helicopter's position was guide enough.

Lawrence's Cadillac was ahead of him. At first it appeared to be empty, then there was a flurry of movement inside.

"Stay out of sight," Mr. Potter said.

"Watch yourself. Be careful," Jack whispered.

Mr. Potter opened the door and got out, tossing his jacket on the seat, turning out his trouser pockets so that Burgess could see that he was unarmed. Raising his head, Jack watched him walk unhurriedly toward the big car. Then the door opened and Janet stumbled out, Janet with her blouse ripped from shoulder to waist, her skirt slipping over her hips because the belt had been torn open.

She stood motionless, watching Mr. Potter approach, her immense dark eyes wide and fixed. And behind her was Burgess, a revolver in his hand. He shoved it against Janet's back.

"Don't come any closer or she gets it."

"He means it, Hiram," Janet said warningly.

Inch by inch, Jack lifted his head, the automatic in his hand. He couldn't use it without endangering the girl.

"I haven't a gun," Mr. Potter said quietly. He took a slow step forward. Another slow step. He watched Burgess's eyes, hot and fevered, saw the thick hand closed over the revolver, saw him sway slightly as he stood barricaded by the girl's slim body.

"We ran out of gas," Janet said and reached down to pull up the skirt which had fallen to her knees.

"Don't move," Burgess warned her sharply.

Something in his voice betrayed that he was close to the breaking point. Janet stood motionless, her eyes on Mr. Potter's. His own flickered. He wanted her to move aside but she couldn't move. The muzzle of the gun was hot against her bare back.

"Hiram," she said quietly, her body rigid, only her eyes alive, "I don't believe Burgess killed Jake Stendel."

"Of course not," he agreed. "All he did was try to protect himself by putting the glass back in Stendel's room. He hoped there were fingerprints on it."

Janet, still watching Mr. Potter, screamed, "Look out! A rattler!"

At the moment when Burgess, his nerves quivering, whirled around, Mr. Potter leaped for Janet, flung her on the ground, and tackled Burgess at the knees. They struck ground together.

Mr. Potter strained to reach Burgess's right hand, which held the revolver, while Burgess brought his left fist down with a smashing blow on the unprotected face. Jack jumped out of the car, but he could not shoot without hitting Mr. Potter.

As Burgess brought his knee up, Mr. Potter flung himself to one side, clinging to that right arm. Slowly he began to twist it behind Burgess's back, the veins standing out on his forehead, while Burgess struck and struck again at the exposed face.

Jack reached Janet, shoved her into the back seat of the Buick. "Keep down," he ordered her.

The two bodies on the ground thrashed. Both Mr. Potter's hands were on Burgess's right arm, pulling it slowly, inexorably behind his back, but he had no protection from the terrible pounding the left hand was giving him.

Cowering in the back of the car, Janet watched, appalled. She had never before seen men fight. Jack kept circling them, gun in hand, waiting for an opening, unable to shoot.

Then Burgess screamed once and fell limp. As Mr. Potter tried to straighten up, Jack kicked the revolver out of reach and helped him to his feet. He stood swaying, his face bleeding.

"I broke his arm," he said breathlessly. "We'll need help to get him back."

Jack played a tattoo on the horn and came back to look without sympathy at the young man who lay unconscious, his arm twisted at an improbable angle. In the back of the car Janet was crying, tears rolling down her cheeks. Jack handed her the skirt that had fallen off, felt under his lapel for a safety pin—Molly, he said, was always coming apart —and poured cold water for her. Then he went back to stare at Burgess.

"Do you still have that flask of brandy in your car?"

"Yes, but the poor devil will be in agony when he comes out of it. Let him stay unconscious as long as we can. I had to do it," he said apologetically.

A car pulled up behind the Buick and two uniformed men tumbled out and came to look at the man on the ground, then at Mr. Potter.

"It must," one of them said, "have been quite a scrap."

"His arm is broken. Be careful," Mr. Potter warned him.

The trooper gave him a curious look. "In your place, I wouldn't give a damn. He's the killer, isn't he?"

"One of them. He killed Dr. Mourner and Noah Ponders, tried to throw me into the canyon and then to send my car and me to eternity."

"Nice guy." The two men hoisted Burgess into the back of the police car. "A right nice guy. Can you drive yourself back?"

"I'll drive," Jack said.

"Is the girl all right?"

Janet, who had been hastily making herself presentable, said, "I'm all right. Honestly. He didn't—hurt me. He was just getting—amorous when you came."

Jack helped Mr. Potter into the back seat, started the car and turned it over bumpy ground. Slowly he fell in line behind the police car. Overhead, the helicopter rose, circled once, and disappeared into the blue of the sky.

"You're bleeding," Janet said, "and I haven't anything —I gave Burgess my handkerchief. His was dirty and I was afraid he'd infect that cut lip."

Mr. Potter, Jack thought, had got himself quite a girl. He glanced briefly in the rear-view mirror but they were not talking, they were not even looking at each other. They sat very close together, their hands locked.

18

THEY HANDLE things efficiently in big hotels. When Janet, Jack Smith, and Mr. Potter returned to the hotel, only one police officer accompanied them and he was in plainclothes. Fortunately there was no one in the elevator when they went up as neither Mr. Potter's face nor Janet's clothing could have stood much scrutiny.

The plainclothesman accompanied Janet to her room, looked around, and then stationed himself patiently in the hall to wait while she dressed.

Jack watched while Mr. Potter tore off collar and tie and set to work to repair damages. As he reached for his jacket, the younger man helped ease his arm into it.

"Quite a scrap," he said. He looked in surprise at Mr. Potter's slight frame. He didn't give the appearance of a man who could stand up to the kind of beating he had taken; certainly not the man to have tackled Burgess single-handed. The latter could give him forty pounds, he had a longer reach, and he was nearly ten years younger. Always a mistake, Jack reminded himself, to try to size up people too fast. Adams had warned him repeatedly.

"I guess that's that," Mr. Potter said as he adjusted his tie.

"You'd better have a drink before you try anything more."

"Not yet. I'd like you to get all of them down here, if you can manage it."

"I'll manage it."

The telephone rang and Mr. Potter reached for it.

"This is Bertha Christie," said a rather unsteady voice at the other end of the line.

"Where are you?"

In a drugstore in the center of town. Would he come for her?

"I'm on my way." He explained briefly to Jack, started for the door, turned back. "Get them here and keep them here. That sounds a bit high-handed but O'Toole fixed it with the local authorities to give me a reasonably free hand."

Traffic was heavy and Mr. Potter drove slowly, looking for the drugstore the nurse had described. As he approached, a car slid away from the curb and he moved in. For a moment he looked around the crowded drugstore, his heart sinking. He must have made a mistake. Then from around a table displaying cosmetics, Christie cautiously poked her head, recognized him, and came to meet him almost at a run, her arms filled with packages. She was white and shaking.

"I'm so glad—so glad—"

He took a closer look at her. "Have you had breakfast?"

She shook her head and he put her into the car and drove on, hunting for a suitable restaurant, ignoring her protests. "Later," he said as she began to talk. "First you are going to eat. You are one of the few levelheaded people in this whole group, Miss Christie, and I can't have you losing control. We'll pile this stuff of yours in the back of the car."

"I don't want any of it. Stationery, soap, powder, perfume—I had to keep buying things so I could stay there without someone wondering why."

He ordered for her and, though she protested at the size of the meal, she ate it all, fruit and cereal, eggs and toast and bacon. When she poured her third cup of coffee she looked across at him, the color back in her cheeks.

"Now tell me what happened to you."

"I was nearly killed and I guess I panicked. I ran away. But now, of course, I've got to go back and face the music, but I didn't want to go alone. Frankly, I didn't dare go alone."

"You won't be alone."

She had got up rather early and had gone to take a bath. She had placed a small radio on the washstand beside the tub. She was feeling rather happy for some reason and she wanted some gay music. Then the door had opened.

"How could anyone get in? Had you left the room door unlocked?"

"The keys were just the same," she said. "We noticed it yesterday when he brought up a package for me and unlocked my door by mistake with his own key."

"Burgess Holman." His tone was steadying.

She nodded. Once more the color faded. "He came right into the bathroom, looking wild. He saw that radio and tried to throw it into the tub."

She lifted the coffee cup and drained it. Her voice was steady when she spoke again. "It was—unbelievable. But I knew he meant to kill me. All that saved me was that he wasn't co-ordinating and I was quicker. I pushed him out of the room and put a chair under the doorknob while I dressed. Then I went out. All I wanted to do was to get away, to be safe. I walked and walked until I found a drugstore big enough so that I could duck around counters and keep out of sight. Then I began buying things. At last I realized that this couldn't go on. Something had to be done. Burgess isn't safe any longer, Mr. Potter. So I knew I had to go back. Only, you see, I was afraid. So I called you."

He explained briefly what had happened and she cried out in horror. "Was Miss Grant badly hurt?"

"No, he was just beginning to make a real nuisance of himself when we got there."

"I'm glad. She's so beautiful I couldn't bear to have her hurt. And she is so terribly in love with you. We talked on the plane coming out."

As they drew into the parking lot he took a searching look at her. She was still pale but she was composed. "You understand, don't you, that this is going to be unpleasant."

She nodded. "At least I'm glad that Burgess won't be there. I couldn't bear to see him after all the terrible harm he has done. I kept wondering about him from the beginning, of course; or at least after I knew for sure that Damon hadn't killed his grandfather. But there was someone else in it, wasn't there?"

"There was someone else, Miss Christie."

"I've gone over it and over it, wondering who could be eliminated. Of course, Mr. Lawrence was in Santa Barbara on business."

"Actually we don't know where he was at the time of Mr. Stendel's murder. His Santa Barbara alibi has blown up in his face."

"Mr. Lawrence!" The nurse was genuinely surprised. "You know, of all her husbands, he is the one who dislikes her least."

For the first time in hours Mr. Potter laughed wholeheartedly.

"Then I thought about Mr. Morris because he kept coming around, but always when Mr. Lawrence was away. As if he knew in advance. And finally I began to suspect even Mrs. Lawrence herself because she was always afraid her father would find out about that marriage. He had the strongest objection to gambling. And perhaps she thought —well, when he was gone, there would be nothing to fear. And yet I don't believe Mr. Morris ever intended to expose her, just frighten her."

"Why not?"

"Well," Christie said practically, "if Mrs. Lawrence lost her income, so would he. There wouldn't be any more profit in it and he has always been a very sensible man."

"He was running a double bluff, Miss Christie. He made her believe he'd never got the divorce, that her marriages with Knox and Lawrence were bigamous. He was never legally married to her at all. He had a wife living at the time. Actually, he still has."

As they got out of the car at the hotel she said, "You know who it is, don't you?"

"I think so. I'm going up to see all of them now. If you'd care to come along, say, in ten minutes—"

She hesitated. "Do you mind very much if I come with you? I'm not usually silly but, somehow, I don't especially want to be alone right now."

He tucked her hand under his arm. "There is nothing more for you to fear, Miss Christie. We're going to wind this affair up now."

"How can you be so sure that they will be waiting for you?"

"Jack Smith is taking care of that. For all his seraphic look he is an extremely competent and intelligent young man. He came here to represent Mr. Roland Adams."

"Then it really is all over," she said in relief. "Mr. Adams doesn't make mistakes."

When Mr. Potter stopped at his door her hand tightened on his arm. He smiled at her encouragingly. "A few unpleasant moments, but it has to be done, you know."

When he entered the room he found it crowded. The Smiths stood close together by the window, with Janet beside them. The trooper who had been left to guard her leaned against the wall close to the door, watching them all curiously. Damon and his father sat side by side on a couch. Winifred Lawrence lay on Mr. Potter's bed, propped up on pillows, her face ravaged, her eyes never leaving Lawrence who sat in a straight chair, smoking and looking at the floor. Sunk in the most comfortable chair in the room, Morris watched them all with a kind of sardonic amusement.

When they caught sight of Christie there was an outburst of exclamations. Damon almost ran to take her in his arms, hugging her.

"Thank heaven!"

The nurse appeared to be calm enough, her face was disciplined, but one hand still clutched Mr. Potter's sleeve.

"Where have you been?" Winifred asked shrilly. "You had us scared half out of our wits. And I needed you."

"I ran away," Christie told her. "Burgess tried to electrocute me this morning and I was frightened. So I ran away until I could think it over and decide what to do."

"Don't be ridiculous," Winifred said. "How can you tell an outrageous story like that? You're just trying to hurt us as a family. You always have. You haven't fooled me a bit. Not a bit. You always hated me because you were in love with my husband."

As Lawrence started to protest she went on feverishly, "Not you, of course, James. It was Damon. Because he was so good-looking." Her voice rose gloatingly. "You wouldn't believe it now, would you?"

"Mother!" At Damon's unleashed fury, Mr. Potter gave him a sharp look but Winifred did not pay any attention.

"You've plotted to destroy me, haven't you, Christie? All that ugly story about father being murdered. It wasn't true. You never found that glass in his room. It wasn't there."

It was the stillness that made her look around, her jaw dropping.

"How do you know that?" Mr. Potter asked quietly. "Lawrence, stay where you are!"

"This," Lawrence said, "is where I get out."

"Stay put, brother," the trooper said easily.

"Winifred isn't my wife. Morris told me this morning. I'm getting out now. He said he never divorced her."

"There couldn't be a divorce," Mr. Potter explained. "Morris already had a wife; he still has. Woman named Cathy Binks. He was never legally married to Winifred."

"Do you know what you are talking about?" Lawrence asked.

"You see?" Winifred cried. "I told you to stick to me, that it would be all right. You see?"

"I know what I'm talking about," Jack Smith said. "I got the information direct from Mexico. By the way, I'd better explain my position here. In a sense, I represent Ro-

204

land Adams's law firm."

Morris got easily to his feet. "Then I'd better be getting along. I'm not concerned in this. I am no longer connected with the Stendel tribe."

"Five people have been killed," Mr. Potter told him, "and four other attempts at murder have been made. And you sparked the whole thing, by demanding so much money that the price became too steep. You aren't an easy man to kill, but if Stendel died the worst of the risk would be over. And, like Macbeth, the first crime simply opened the way for the others.

"Winifred was frantic. She wanted the money, she wanted Lawrence, and you threatened her on both counts. But she didn't dare tell Lawrence, she didn't dare tell her son, who would take a dim view of murder. But there was her nephew, Burgess, who, like herself, was bitter, driven by a sense of injustice, and aware that, if his past record were to be exposed, he would probably lose his share of the money.

"As your bite got bigger and bigger, Winifred began to break and she sent for Miss Christie, who always came when she was in trouble. Then her father became ill. There was no reason, apparently, why he should not go on living for years, but Winifred knew an opportunity when she saw one. She went into his room at night and put white arsenic in his drinking glass. Later she went to retrieve the glass and met Burgess in the hall.

"He made her break down and tell him what she had done. He took the glass from her, intending to keep it in case any question arose, so that he himself would be in the clear. But he had drunk himself practically blind and in his confused state he left the glass in Stendel's room when he went in to verify the fact that he had been murdered.

"When Miss Christie went in she found her patient dead and realized by the signs that he had been poisoned. For once in her life she let her loyalty to a family cloud her judgment and her integrity as a nurse. She removed the glass, had the contents analyzed, and then—"

"It's not true," Winifred broke in. "It's not true. James darling, can't you see it's not true? She's trying to hurt me and discredit Burgess so Damon can get all the money. Because of his father."

Lawrence stared at her in disbelief. Damon did not look at his mother at all. He sat with his hands loosely clasped between his knees, looking blankly at the wall, a gray pallor under his tan.

Mr. Potter still stood at ease, looking from one to another. "Well, Winifred and Burgess got an unexpected break. Miss Christie had removed the evidence and Dr. Mourner issued a death certificate. But Burgess was in a panic. Murder in theory was one thing; in fact, it was more than he could cope with. He cracked wide open and he tampered with the doctor's brakes, with some confused idea that by killing the man he could eliminate the danger. In the crash that followed, three people died.

"Now Winifred was anxious to get rid of Christie. So anxious that she offered to send her on a long freighter trip for a rest and a sightseeing cruise. But Winifred wasn't a generous woman and Christie was unhappy about the whole situation. She didn't want to take what she thought might be blood money. Instead of going away, she went to work for Dr. Holman and, eventually, told him the truth.

"That's when I came into the picture. Winifred found out that Christie was working for her brother-in-law and she was terrified. She begged her to come out at once, said that her nerves were breaking. And Dr. Holman asked me to come along, not only to keep an eye on Christie but, to find out how much truth there was in her story. You all know what happened. Burgess tried to push Christie into the canyon and got poor Ponders instead."

Lawrence shook his head as though he were punch-drunk.

"James darling," Winifred cried, "you weren't involved. You know you weren't. I didn't want you even to get off the bus that time. And—just in case, you know—I said you had dizzy spells. To cover you. Didn't I? Didn't I?"

"God," he said, his voice muffled. "It was only when Mr. Potter asked about those dizzy spells—and I don't have them—that I began to wonder. Only—I couldn't really take it in—and Winifred didn't get off the bus. I didn't know what to think."

"It was after that," Mr. Potter went on, "that the two of them decided to get rid of me. First Burgess tried to shove me into the canyon; then he drained brake fluid from my car. But he had a run of bad luck. And last night, Winifred took a hand in her own inimitable fashion and put arsenic in my glass of scotch. But I'm a wary bird.

"By that time they were nearly desperate. Christie and I were still around and still dangerous. They didn't know what Christie had done with the glass. Burgess realized that I knew enough about his past activities to end any chance of his getting his inheritance. So, early this morn-ing, Burgess went into Christie's room, saw the radio, and tried to push it into the tub and electrocute her. But Christie is strong and active and she saved herself.

"Then he lured Janet out to Lawrence's car in a mad at-tempt to hold her as hostage until I agreed to withhold my information from Roland Adams."

"Where is Burgess?" Winifred demanded. "He'd tell

you that you are lying. You wouldn't dare say these things if he were here."

"He is now in the hospital, charged with murder."

Winifred stared at him, her eyes wild. "No, no."

The trooper moved toward her.

"Don't touch me!" she screamed. "It wasn't my fault. It was my father's fault. That damnable will. What else could we do?"

Stiff as he was, Mr. Potter reached her before the trooper, grasped her wrist firmly. The trooper removed the compact she was clutching.

"Careful," Mr. Potter said, "I think there is still a lethal dose of arsenic in it."

She went quietly with the trooper who held her arm. She did not look back. She moved like a sleepwalker. Like that other Lady Macbeth, she, too, had bad dreams.

There was a hush in the room and then a collective sigh; everyone moved a little.

It was Christie who spoke first. "What will they do to her?"

"The problem may be handled medically or she may face a first-degree charge. It's out of my hands, Miss Christie. She might have a better chance if she hadn't involved herself with Burgess, but he has nothing to lose now and I can't see him helping to clear her at his own expense."

"Burgess was horrible," Janet said abruptly, "but in a way he wasn't altogether to blame. He was off his head."

Mr. Potter smiled at her. "You're a very forgiving woman."

"She's right, of course," Christie said. "If he'd been normal, I couldn't have coped with him this morning. But he was groggy from a terrible beating. He hardly knew what he was doing."

"I did that." Damon made a sudden rush for the bath-room. When he came back he sank onto the sofa beside his father, limp and white.

Mr. Potter poured him a drink of scotch. "I'm sorry. There really was no other action I could have taken. Some day I hope you'll understand and try to forgive me."

Damon held the glass in a shaking hand. "It wasn't your fault. Nothing else you could do. It's the Maybrick blood. Am I like that, Christie?"

"You're half your father," she said stoutly. "You needn't be afraid of your heritage, Damon. You ought to be proud of it. And your Aunt Helen was one of the sanest women I ever knew."

Again Morris stood up, drifted toward the door.

"Stick around," Mr. Potter advised him. "You'll have to testify. Your blackmail triggered this whole thing. Nothing can clear you of your share of responsibility for this holo-caust." As the gambler started to protest he added, his voice hard, "I've already talked to the authorities. You will stay of your own free will or you'll be held as a material witness. Take your choice."

Morris went out and Lawrence got up, steadying himself against a table. At Mr. Potter's nod he went out quickly.

Jack glanced at his wife. "Come along, Molly. I've got to get hold of R. A. and make a complete report before the police talk to him. You're quite a guy, Mr. Potter. You ought to feel pleased with yourself."

Damon went out between his father and the nurse.

" 'Pleased'?" Mr. Potter repeated. "I'm wondering what I'm going to say to Dr. Holman when I call him to report."

"You know," Janet said unexpectedly, "I wouldn't be surprised if he was already prepared to hear it. After all, this is a field in which he's an authority, but he couldn't bring himself to accuse his own son and yet he couldn't permit him to go on. He made you the *deus ex machina*."

The telephone rang. It was Weston calling from New York. He'd just found out that Lawrence had an alibi for the time of Stendel's killing. He'd been in Santa Barbara but not with a business acquaintance. He had been with a Frieda Tutter. Long-standing affair but of a mild sort. She said what he really wanted was a mother and probably Winifred had served the purpose as well as anyone.

"Somehow I doubt that." Rapidly, Mr. Potter brought him up to date.

"I thought from the beginning that Burgess and Winifred were involved," Weston said in a tone of satisfaction. "Because of those car accidents they had been involved in."

"You," Mr. Potter told him, "have a one-track mind."

At Weston's comment Mr. Potter laughed and set down the telephone. "Weston says my mind hasn't been on the job."

"I'm your job," Janet said.

The telephone rang again. "It's Cass," Mr. Potter told her in surprise, putting the telephone in her hand. "Here in Las Vegas. I never thought he meant to come."

After a few moments Janet said, "Hold on while I ask him." She looked at Mr. Potter. "Cass just got here. He asked whether I'd trapped you into proposing yet. If I've had any luck, he wants us to celebrate tonight."

"Will you marry—"

"Yes," she said promptly.

Some time later she drew back, aware of the noises coming from the telephone. "Good heavens, I forgot Cass." She held the telephone to her ear, laughed. "He said that he got the message. He'll met us at seven. Just the same, you had better do something about those bruises, Hiram. Cass will think I had to beat you into submission."

"Later," he promised. "Later. There's plenty of time. Come here."